From Here

Vincent Miller

Contents

Prologue

W arm, sunny, laughter, driving, and fighting over what music to put on was our routine anywhere we drove to, when it came to my grandmother, mother, and I. As we drove down the road ahead of us, on our way to a family friend's house; that was in the middle of nowhere, it was like we had done this thousands of time - well in reality we probably did this like a million times before, but who's counting.

"Look at the horses, Kyla" said my mother from the drivers seat. Sometimes just to annoy her, I'd ask a stupid question like: "Where? I don't see it".

Knowing very well I was trying to annoy her she said, "You know what side of the windows, to look at".

"Gosh, Kyla. The horses are on the right," my grandmother told me; just before I went back to annoy my mother.

Both, my grandmother and mother, were everything to me. It was just us three since I like was four years-old. We did everything together from cleaning our small two bedroom house, to cooking, to doing almost anything. All we needed was each other and no one else. Even though my mom had been single since her divorce from my dad, when he went to prison, and claimed all she needed was me, still I worried for her.

We were only a couple minutes from the house. I turned towards the windows of the car to see the scenery. Oh, how nice it's be to get away from the world. The blue sky with clouds, the yards of some type of trees, and everything that went by us as we drove, these were the moments that I loved to be in.

Still looking at everything that was outside of the car, I heard my mother mutter something I couldn't quite make out. I think she said shit or crap, something between those words. "What's going on" said my grandmother. "I don't know. I wanted to turn to the right on the stop sign that we passed but nothing; the car won't let me turn," my mother told her; still keeping her eyes on the road ahead.

"Try turning on the road to your left, that's coming ahead," directed my grandmother. Following her directions, my mother turning the steering wheel. Nothing. The car still kept on going straight. Starting to grow wary, my mother tried pulling at her emergency brakes. Nothing. The car only allowed us to continue going straight.

Absolutely nothing happed.

"What are we going to do now?" I asked, it seemed as if it was the only thing I could ask. I remember maybe thirty-five minutes pass or so, yet seemed like a couple hours to us. My grandmother and mother, appeared to have the same thought flash their minds, to unlock our seatbelts. Picking up what they were doing, I copied them; freeing myself from my seatbelt behind the front passengers seat. Bringing my attention too my grandmother and mother, in the front in the car, it took me a couple of seconds to register was was occurring. Their seatbelts would not unbuckle. They struggled to pull, but it wouldn't budge. In this moment, all I could think about was how lucky we would have been if we had something to cut the seat belts. Maybe scissors, a knife, or anything so that they be free from what was restraining them in their seats.

The look the went by my mother and grandmother, is one that I have only seen when something serious was going on that they didn't know what to do or make out. Fear. Concern. Sensing my eyes on them, they turned to look at me. "Kyla, you know we love you, and will always love you," said my mom. "I know that mom, but we have to get out of the car, before we hit that mountain that's coming up ahead," I told them both as I shifted my gaze from my grandmother and mother.

"We can't get free of our seatbelts, Kyla" my grandmother told me in a cold voice.

"No, no, no. We are all getting out of this car! We have too!" I began to yell.

Getting filled with fear and adrenaline, I begun to climb over to them from the back seats to try to free them. I pulled, and tugged on the seat belts but it did not seem to do nothing. Then, I tried opening their doors thinking that they could somehow free themselves by pulling the seatbelts to all their limit and up from the car.

Their doors would not open... Their windows would not open...

There were trapped in their seats, while I was free to move.

It all happened so quickly. My mother and grandmother yelling at my stuff of having a long life to live, full with experiences, and love; telling me that they loved me. Suddenly, I was instructed to jump out. Looking up to see my mother and grandmother, I saw scared to hear what they were going to say.

"We promise to be fine. We have our seatbelts, and the car has airbags. We'll both be fine. But Kyla, you, have to get out. Do we hear me, get out of the car," my mother directed me in a stern voice.

"But I don't want to leave you guys," I said as my lips quivered and unshed tears in my eyes that blurred my vision.

"I know you don't, but you have too. We promise we'll be fine. When have we broken a promise, huh?" my grandmother told me in a soft voice.

Starting to believe them, I carried my body to the side of the car in the back where I had been mere hours ago; opening the door. Looking back at their faces for one last time, believing that they'd be fine, I jumped from the car. Everything was not the same afterwards...

Chapter 1 - From, then on

POV: Kyla Bower ~

Life sucks.

Now. Even more.

Not that life ever stopped.

As soon as school, ended I grabbed and put all my belongings into my backpack and got my ass out of that place. I use to enjoy and look forward to being at school; now it's just a mediocre act I do everyday, expect then no one was giving me looks of pity, and sadness. I hate pity and sadness from others. But now, it's all what others seems to be giving me at school, stores, everywhere.

When they were still here, everything was good. I could not have asked for better.

I am just sick of everything.

Walking back from the back of school near the alleyway, I plug in my earphones to my phone to zone out my horrible reality. I listen to 'Don't

Tell My Mom' by Reneé Rapp. Before I even realize it, I'm singing along to the song:

Don't worry about me, just worry about you

So, don't tell my mom, I'm fallin' apart

She hurts when I hurt, my scars are her scars

How funny. I can't even tell my mom anything, now anyways.

Within seconds, I'm in front of the small diner I work at. My mother, grandmother and I use to come here almost all weekends, sometimes even weekdays too, if we didn't feel like cooking. I walk in and I'm greeted by Gina, the owner; she's been nice throughout since my mother and grandmother died. "How's it going, mija?" Gina asks me. Shitty. "Fine, schools is school", I tell her.

I steal a glance of her on my left when I'm at the counter tying my apron, and she has a small frown on her face. "¿Sabes que me puedes decir cualquier cosa, no?" (You know you can tell me anything, no?) she questions. "Ya lo se, Gina, gracias" (I know that, Gina, thanks), I tell her and make my way to a booth with an old couple who just walked in with menus in my hand.

After a six and a half shift with a ten minute break, I'm beat. Working with food, sometime is fun, other days not so fun. Today, it was not so fun. I had to deal with so many people, annoying people at it too. I had to help this one group of girls, who seemed my age by taking their order; they took so long to just order a couple of milkshakes. I swear. Done with my shift, I notice taking out my phone the time, 10:37 pm. It could not have passed by any faster, note the sarcasm. With that I take my leave, from the back door where employee lockers are and start to head home.

Once I'm in front of my apartment door, I get my keys from my backpack to open the door when I notice something slip out. Now with the door open, I turn to retrieve when had fallen to see that its a picture of all three of us. My grandmother, mother and I. Standing to my full height of 5'2, I look down at the picture in my hands; in the picture I seem so happy with them on both of my sides, smiling as they look at me. I remember thing day, it was so unexpected. My mom had woken my grandmother and I at 5 in the morning to take us to an aquarium. Mom loved traveling to places and having an experience with the us. My grandmother loved spending time together. In the picture, we were complete, together.

After the accident, we were separated. I was lonely. From, then on, I was left with nothing and no one by my side.

I get in my room, the only room in the apartment, and drop on my mattress which is on the floor after letting my backpack fall to the floor. I feel so lonely without them with me. We were all we had to each other, no one else. In a couple of minutes, I feel my eyelids become heavy and my mind drifting to sleep.

I just hope tomorrow, is better than today.

-

-

-

Author's note: I hope you all enjoy this chapter. I am going to try to update it to the best of my ability. I am so sorry it took so long, but please have in mind I am a college student, and at times it can get hard to update with me being busy.

Thank you for reading!

Chapter 2 - No way is this happening!

~ POV: Kyla Bower ~

When I wake up, I feel the light shining to my eyes which causes me to wake up. Contemplating whether I should go to school or not, I stick to the choice that I always regret making; going to school. Turning to look at the clock on my bed stand table, I look to see that it is six twenty four in the morning, I guess it's time to get up... not that I want too. Nevertheless, I grab my clothes for the day: a white t-shirt with pink and blue stripes, a pair of blue baggy jeans, and my old beaten up Van's.

Once all dressed up, I grab my backpack and keys to head out of my apartment. On my way to school, take in my surrounds sensing how calm it is, rather than the usual rowdy and busy traffic that happens in the mornings.

Then in almost 30 minutes of walking, I make it to school. Shoreville High School. Just as I'm passing the open gates of school, the bell rings. Rushing over to my locker and getting my books, I make my way to Pre-Calculus, my least favorite class.

Going inside the classroom, with my classmates would also don't understand any the teacher has been saying for the past 20 minutes, Riley decides to start talking to me. Riley, considers herself my friend; we use to hangout every now and then, but since I've lost my grandma and mom, I prefer to keep people at a distance. Scared to lose more people that I care about.

"Do you even understand what Mr. Ramirez is explaining?" Riley asks me in a whisper.

"He's explain electric current and that one formula and no I don't understand," I tell her in a whisper and point to the board.

"At least I'm not the only one," she responds to me in a boring tone.

Suddenly the phone of Mr. Ramirez's desk rings, snapping the attention of most of the class to the front. Walking to the phone, Mr. Ramirez picks it up and listens to what is being said on the other line, whilst looking around the class. When his eyes land on me, he ends the call with an okay and a thank-you.

"Ms. Bower, your being needed in the administration office"

Picking up my backpack from the floor and making my way to the class door, the class erupts in a childish a fit of "I wonder what she did" or "She's in trouble" remarks, making me roll my eyes. Once at the administration office, and being told by the secretary to be seated til the principal calls me, I start to get anxious and wondering if they found out I live by myself. Then the door to the principal's office opens, and I'm being summoned to enter. Sitting down in the chair opposite from the principal's desk, I begin to pick on the skin around my nails; it has been a habit of mine when I'm nervous.

As the principal sits down, I see that in her eyes is an emotion that I cannot distinguish between sadness, or concern. "Ms. Bower, I have been informed that as a minor you have been living alone for awhile now," she informs me.

No way is this happening! Now at any other moment, it had to be now or all time. Shit! "I have already notify CPS, of your situation and they will be coming shortly to pick you up, and discuss somethings with you along with your grandmother's will. I am very sorry of your loss," the principal hands me a box of tissues as she finishes what she is telling me. I come up with a lie, anything to get her off my back. "Thank you, but I've been living with an old friend... but how did you know that my grandmother died. She's been dead for at least 7 months already with my mom," I tell her the last part in a low voice.

"I'm sorry to hear that Ms. Bower, truly, however I was not aware of that. When I was on the phone with CPS, they mentioned a grandmother of yours from your father's side," she tells me in soft tone.

Dumbfounded with this new information I let her know that I have not seen this grandmother of mine, I guess, since I was 4 years old. I barely remember her. "I'm sorry, Ms. Bower, but there is nothing I can do. My hands are tied," she ends just as she gets a knock on her office and the door opening to show a woman and man with badges.

~~~

At the CPS, Child Protective Services Department, I am told to sit and wait along with "we will let you know when there is any information we can give you". Hour and hours pass by and I am still waiting for them to let me know of any information, anything. As I hear a door opening and I turn see where the noise came from, I see the woman that was with me early come my way.

"Hello, Ms. Bower. I did not introduce myself earlier when we met but I am Lisa Sanders, your social worker that is working on your case. You can call me however you'd like. I just came to give you good news that we were able to get in contact with lawyer who worked on your grandmother's will," Lisa announces to me.
~~~

This is a lot to process.

"Okay? What's going to happen to me in the meantime?" I question her since she has given me no information about myself.

"The lawyer said that he will be sending a car for you to stay at a hotel in while he gets some paper work ready. He almost told me to tell you that tomorrow in the morning he will be going to the hotel to do a rundown on some important subjects that need to be addressed and to be ready by 8 in the morning".

~~~

At the hotel room and alone, I feel my body heavy. Sprawling out on the bed, I lay on my back and stare at the ceiling think of everything that happened today with school, the principal, CPS, the social worker, the will and lawyer. It has been a hectic day that I want this to end. With a final thought before I fall asleep, I think of my grandma and mom, and how I am all alone.

I certainly did not think anything crazy was going to happen.
~~~

Chapter 3 - Stuck at the Office

~ POV: Richard Bower ~

Being stuck in the office, having to wait on some potential business partner was not what I wanted to do at on a late Wednesday night. I can just leave them, it is not like they're the company's business partner yet. I dismiss that idea as quickly as came into my mind. I took over this company, Bwell Inc., after being released from prison where I was wrongful accused of fraud that I never committed. The company I had worked for before, R & R, had schemed a fake fraud and blamed it on me, just so that they could get ride of me before I outted them to the all media networks of them illegally working with a substances and making business deals to steal percentages of their earning.

No one believed me. When I told people, I did not do it, they turned a blind eye on me. They all believed the lies.

I lost everything and almost everyone.

My five sons would visit me at the being. They too hoped that I would be released early, however I was not. A couple of months later, I stopped visiting although they would call time to time. The mother of only daughter cut off all contact with me when I was first put in prison. The last time I was her was when she was barely 4 years old.

Kyla.

I haven't seen or hear from her or her mother for the last 12 years.

Deep in thought, I barely registered that my cellphone was ringing. I pick it up to see that the caller ID is unknown. Having this feeling that it's important, I pick it up.

"Hello, is this by any chance Mr. Richard Bower, speaking?" the person on the other line asks.

"Yes, this Richard Bower. How may I help you?" I ask attempting to sound confident and not confused.

"I am Mr. Larry Haydes. I work for the Trukin law firm. It's sorry to tell you this, but I must inform you that your mother, Mrs. Isabel Bower, has died. I am very sorry for your lost," he tells me in a sounding much softer than before.

Silence.I am silent for a couple minutes, digesting that my mother has died.

"Mr. Bower, I am your mother's lawyer. I wanted to let you know that tomorrow her will is scheduled to read. I have to let you know that your attendance along with your children's is required. With your permission, may it be held at one of mom's estate?"

"Yes, of course. I understand, I will also be there"

"Thank you. Again, I am very sorry for your lost" he tells me at last before the call is ended.

Silence.

I feel treats starting to brim by eyes.

Then I'm crying.

How could my mother have died? She was the only person that I had contacted with, while in I was falsely accused in prison. She was there, when no one was.

I already miss you deep...

Chapter 4 - Seen Her Somewhere

Waking up, I'm disoriented of where I am. This isn't my room. A couple minutes pass, and I recall all the events of yesterday: school, principal, social worker, will, and lawyer. I'm knocked out of my thoughts, by a knock on the hotel room's door. Rushing to open the door, I'm greeted with a middle-aged man. I look at the man up and down and notice that the man is light skinned, tall, has an expensive looking suit on, dress shoes, glasses and dark brown hair with some grey hairs.

"Um, how can I help you?" I ask the man in front of me. The man extends his hand and says, "I'm Mr. Larry Haydes. I work for the law firm, R & R, whose working on your grandmother, Mrs. Isabel Bower's will," he lets me know.

"I am also here to take you to your grandmother's estate, where the will reading, will be read. We will be leaving in thirty five minutes. I advise you start getting ready, I shall wait for you in the lobby," he tells me and walks away to where I assume is the elevator.

With Mr. Haydes gone, I start to get my clothes to take a shower. I did not bring much things with me, since I hardly had anythings while I was staying at the apartment. I also make a mental note to call Gina, my manager, to let her know that I will not be going to work anymore and of my current situation. Once out of the shower, I quickly stuff all my belonging into the duffel bag I brought, which mostly contains a few articles of clothings, and mostly books that I've managed to buy at thrift stores for a couple cents. They were such a steal.

Once I'm in the lobby, Mr. Haydes stands from where he was seated and makes his way to the entrance of the hotel, soon motioning for me to follow him. Outside of the hotel, he informs me that the hotel has already been paid, and to not worry at all. We then proceed to get into a nice black car, where a driver awaits us. Mr. Haydes goes to sit in the front passenger side, and me going to sit in the back seat behind the driver.

"How long is it to get to my grandmother's estate?" I ask Mr. Haydes, once situated.

"I will take us about an hour and a half to get there. In the meantime, be calm and comfortable."

How I suppose to be calm and comfortable?

~~~

An hour and a half later, the car pulls up to a beautiful mansion. The mansion is white and has a fountain in the front. It is so beautiful!

Getting out of the car, Mr. Haydes and I stand in front of the doors, me slightly behind him. A man opens the door for us, who I assume works for the house, and tells us to follow him. He leads us to an office, and says to wait for moment where the others with come. Taking a seat I begin to think.
~~~

I wonder who the 'others' are?

-

~ POV: Richard Bower ~

I'm in my room, waiting for Mr. Haydes to come when someone knocks on the door. Letting out a 'come in', Leo, one of the house workers says that everyone is in the main office downstairs along with Mr. Haydes. After a "thank you for letting me know", I make way downstairs to the main office to hear the reading.

At the door of the office with my hand on the doorknob, I take a deep breath and open the door. Looking around the office, I see my sons from my oldest to youngest: Christian, Elijah, Levi, Mason, and Ryder. To the side is Mr. Haydes, where he seems to be looking at the bookshelf speaking to himself? I go to greet my sons, I've missed them; even if the would visit me while I was in prison, it wasn't the same. I go up to each other them and embrace them in a hug. After hugging them, we stay quiet taking in our presence.

I turn to direct my attention to Mr. Haydes, his back facing me; I hear snippets of small conversation going one between Mr. Haydes and some-one else. The voice seems to be of a girl.

"Mr. Haydes, I believe we are all present to go forth with the reading," I brake the conversation. Mr. Haydes, then moves to the side, bring to view a girl sitting down.

I stay stuck in my place. This can't be... Kyla, my baby.

My Kyla. I stare at the young girl in front of me. She looks so much like her mother, Mary. Her tan skin, wavy hairy, dark colored eyes... She looks so beautiful; there is not a trace of the four year old that would run around the living room yelling "daddy, daddy, come here!" She's grown up so much in the twelve years of me not seeing her. I remember when she would only come to me when she wasn't feeling good, or sad. When she would laugh so much that she's old her stomach pretending that it hurt from all the laughing, or when she'd smile so big at me that her dimples would pop out, one being a little deeper than the other.

Suddenly, someone clearing their throat is what snaps me out of my memory lane trance. I don't care who it was that cleared their throat, I go back to looking at Kyla.

She looks back at my with wide eyes for a few seconds, and then moves her gaze to the boys. She must be stunned. I notice that she grows nervous and uncomfortable as she shifts in her seat. "Fuck," I hear Kyla mutter, while the boys are about to sit down. I am the last to sit as I'm still shock to see my baby after so many years. My sons and daughters and here.

"Who is she?" Mason whispers.

"I don't know, but I feel like I've seen her somewhere," Elijah answer back.

"Me too" is followed by Christian and Ryder.

Mr. Haydes goes to sit at the desk. Kyla is seated by herself to the left, the boys and I are seated to the right.

"Okay, we shall start the reading of Mrs. Isabel Bower's will"

~

~

Chapter 5 - The Will

"Okay, we shall start the reading of Mrs. Isabel Bower's will"

~~~

My dad is here.

My dad, Richard Bower is here. In the same, space as me.

When Mr. Haydes moved and I saw my dad, I didn't know how I felt; I was flabbergast. I was probably even more than flabbergast. He just stared at me. He didn't say anything, not even a peep. He is in front of me after twelve years, and didn't address me in any form. He wasn't there, he didn't contact me; never called, sent letter, anything. It's like he forgot about me, and mom, and he's acting like he's seen a ghost.

What the hell is happening. I question while remaining quiet.

""If you are all here and listening to this from my lawyer, it is because I am now gone. I wish I could have seen the day that my youngest son, and grandchildren are all together alas. My son, Richard, although you have gone through an extremely difficult hardship of being in prison for some-
~~~

thing that you did not commit; I hope you know that I always believed in you. I know that you did not commit fraud. You have always been honest, loyal, and responsible with everything that you have have sought to do. I remember as a child, you'd go after either your after or I to see you could observe or learn from us. When you went on to college, I knew you were going to be bright; then, you went on to work and you were and are still going to be success. It pains me that I will not be able to see what you do in the future," says Mr. Haydes.

I look around the room and set my gaze on my father. Looking at him, I see his eyes red and his cheeks tearstained. Then, I see the boys behind him with clenched jaws as if they're not trying to cry. The youngest looking boy has glassy eyes. I guess he feels that I'm looking at him because he stares by dead in the eye, looks at my face and faces away from me.

I feel so out of place here. I don't belong here. I shouldn't even be here. Most of all, I basically don't even know anyone. Who even are these boys? What are they doing here? and why do they seem close with Richard?

It doesn't even matter to me.

""To my grandsons', Christian, Elijah, Levi, Mason, and Ryder: you are the best things that have come into this life. Christian, Elijah, Levi, Mason, and Ryder, I know that you will do great things in the future where it be in your business career in Chris's case, or whatever career you chose to follow, and in life. I would have loved to have some of you graduate, be successful in your future careers, change the world in the way that you all have changed my life. I missed you all when we stopped seeing each other for a while because of the start of the horrible incident with your father. I'm happy that you all stayed together despite everything. My Chris, Lijah, Lev, Mase, and Ry: I love you all dearly and will forever miss you. You have all changed my life in an immense way. You will all do wonderful things in your lives' and greatness,"" states Mr. Haydes as he continues to read the will.

Grandsons.

They're grandsons of my grandmother from my father's side.

Wait...

If their my grandmother's grandsons, and close with dad, just who are they?

"Soon, we will be done with the reading and will be moving on to the logistical part of the Mrs. Isabel Bower's will," Mr. Haydes lets us all know.

""And to Kyla, my granddaughter," starts Mr.Haydes.

"Granddaughter?" questions one of the boys. I think it was Mason, but I'm sure.

They all look at me confused. You're not the only one's that are confused. I raise an eyebrow at them, and return my attention to Mr. Haydes.

""My Kyla, dear, you are special. I knew you were special from the moment I saw you as a baby. It has been so long since I have last seen you; you were less than 5 years old, I believe. You were such a small child, but full of life. Every time you came with your mother, you brought light into any room you entered. You captured everyones attention. I have missed you so much, you have not idea. Your father has also missed you. I tried looking for you, but I had no luck. I knew that your mother, would take good care of you and raise you well. She always was an amazing woman, your mother. Kyla, I would have loved to see you again. I have missed you, I want you to know that you were always in my thoughts. You were never forgotten. My dear, I hope that do not resent your father. Your father always thought about you, as well. He wanted to reach out to you, but did not want to hold you back as you grew up since you were too young. I dream that your father, the rest of the boys, and you grow close. I love you, Kyla, and always missed you,"" and with that Mr. Haydes ends.

I don't really remember much of my paternal grandmother, but from her words she seems like a nice and caring person. She had a lot to say for all of us, even me; even if she didn't see me since I was like 4 years old or around there.

"Now to the logistics of Mrs. Isabel Bower's assets, she has her house in Connecticut and all other houses in other countries to Mr. Richard Bower; the townhouse for Christian in New York; to Elijah, the beach house in Hawaii; Levi, the villa in New Mexico; Mason, the ranch in Oregon; the log cabin for Ryder, and the manor in Pennsylvania for Kyla," Mr. Haydes says.

"What about this estate?" asks Levi.

"I was getting there," responds Mr. Haydes irritated. "As for her money, and financial accounts, each will be distributed to equal amounts to her son, grandsons, and granddaughter. Her wedding ring will be given to Richard, along with her husband's watch, each grandson will be given one of their grandfather's watch, and Kyla will be given all of her remaining jewelry. However, the there are terms in order to obtain these assets; You all must live together for a year in this estate."

What the fuck.

"You must live together. If by any chance one of you, do not comply to live together then neither one of you will receive the following assets, even if it was addressed to you solely. In simple terms, it is either you all take it or no one receives anything," announces Mr. Haydes.

"Wait, so we all have to be in accordance to the terms of the will or else we all get nothing?" questions who I think is Elijah.

"Did you not hear what he just said? It's either we're all together and agree on the terms or neither of our pockets get anything," I answer him a 'dub' tone.

"How could she even put terms like that?" says Mason.

"She can. It's her will, she can put whatever she wants," tells Christian to all of us.

"Besides, who is she and why is she part of grandma's will?" asks Elijah while aiming a pointed finger my way, gaining everyone's eyes on me. How lovely to have all the attention.

This just got even crazier than I could have imagined.

Chapter 6 - Hey?

POV: Kyla Bower ~

"Who are you guys?" I retort to the boys that are near my father's side.

Out of nowhere Mr. Haydes, steps in almost like a human divider between my father and those boys on one side, and me on the other. "I shall step out for a moment to allow you all to discuss your... relationship with other," notes Mr. Haydes before going out the office. Still, before he goes out of the office he shoots a small smile my way, as if a gesture of sympathy. He knows something. I can tell, but what? I turn my attention to the boys and my father.

Looking at all of the boys they all look kind of similar to each other. With silence embracing the space, my father is the first to break it.

"Christian, Elijah, Levi, Mason, and Ryder, why don't you introduce yourselves to her," Richard says.

"Hello, I'm Christian,"" I'm Elijah," "Hi, it's Levi," "Mason," "and my name's Ryder," they all tell me standing close to each other facing me. I shoot my gaze to my father and he does a small gesture for me to also introduce myself. With an eye roll, I do as told to be polite, not because it was my father telling me to do it.

Yet, before I leave the office I do a small wave with my hand to them and say, "Hey? I'm Kyla." They continue to look at me like that should mean anything to them. "Isabel was my grandma... Richard is my father," I fill them in. Then all hell breaks loose.

Questions are asked and statements are thrown around the office like, "Her granddaughter?", "Grandma didn't have a granddaughter", and "How is this possible?"

"It's not that hard to understand... I mean this guy is my father which makes Isabel my grandmother from his side and me her granddaughter," I say by motioning to my father whose near them.

They all stare at me wide-eyed and then slowly turn to my father. "Look boys, I can explain," he directs to them. He turns to face me and takes a couple of steps towards me. "Kyla, can you go give us some privacy to talk. I will call you soon, there's a room two doors down. We'll go to you after talking", he tells me and tries to give me a kiss on the head. Tries being a key word. I move a step back seeing what he's going to do, after moving I see that he was a frown on his face and hides it fast with a small smile.

I make my way towards the door, but before I going out I turn to see the boys and my father. Levi must feel me looking because he gives me a wave, with a small nod I exit the office, going to where my father told me.

What are going to talk about, anyways?

~~~

~ POV: Richard Bower ~
~~~

Once Kyla is out of the office, I return my eyes to the boys. If I would have known Kyla was going to be here, I would have told them beforehand who she was. This is just great! This is exactly how I wanted my youngest child to meet her brothers, note my sarcasm. After telling them to be quiet while I explain them who Kyla, and getting agreements from them I begin.

"Boys, I don't know how to else to explain who she is. I was going to tell you when you all. were younger, but I didn't get a chance too. When I was in prison, I didn't see the need to say anything about her since you all were probably never going to see her again. Kyla, she's... Kyla's my daughter. She's your sister," I break the new news to them.

For a couple minutes, they stay silent. Their silence must mean that they are digesting the news that they have a little sister. Damn it! This was not how they were suppose to find out about one another.

"What do you mean we were probably not going to see her again? When have we ever seen her?" asks Elijah.

"This is the first time we've seen her, I believe, right? Right, dad?" questions Ryder.

"You have met her in the past. When you all were younger, Chris was 13, Elijah 12, Levi 11, Mason 8, and Ryder was 6, I took you guys to the zoo with a little girl, remember? Then, I had lied to you all and your mothers' that I was watching one of my business colleagues daughter; well, she wasn't the daughter of a colleague. She was, is my daughter. You all were together! You all seemed to have a connection with each other. Chris, you carried her. Elijah, you, helped her walk. Levi, you told her jokes. Mason, you played with her. Oh, and Ryder, you held her hand while walking. I just wanted you all to meet each other, I didn't know how to tell you all that I had another child with someone else. Kyla's mother and me, never got married. We were together, when we had her. You're mother's despised me already, I didn't want them to give me a reason to not see you, guys. So

I lied. I lied, and I'm sorry. I'm sorry I never told you all. I just wanted all my children to see each other, and together even if it was a little while," I tell the boys. I look at them with unshed tears in my eyes.

I blink a few time and feel a few tears fall down my face. I haven't said anything to me about what I've just told them about Kyla or even moved. I understand that it is a lot of information to take in for them. They have a sister that they haven't known about for the majority of their lives. It's my fault ultimately for never telling them. I always regretted never telling them, even when they went to visit me in prison over the years.

I just never had the courage to tell my boys about Kyla.

"How old is she, I mean Kyla. How old is Kyla?" Christian asks me.

"She should be sixteen"

"What do you mean 'she should'? You don't know your daughter's own age?" follows Levi.

"I do know. I haven't seen her since she was four. Not once after I went to prison"

"Why didn't you see her? Where has she even been?" questions Ryder to me.

"She's been with her mother, and I never looked to contact Kyla's mother or her to tell her that I was in prison. I let her mother know that we wouldn't see, or hear from me for a long time. Her mother, must have told her I was in prison", I answer them.

"So, let me get this straight. We have a sister that we've never known about til now. Whose in a room a couple of doors down the hallway, and she doesn't;t know about us either?", inputs Ryder, after having listened to me tell them the truth.

"That's correct," I answer honestly. I feel like a weight has been lifted off my shoulder, now that I've told my boys about my baby.

"I truly am sorry for never telling you, boys about her. I understand if it's hard to forgive me. I dot know if I'd even forgive myself" I tell them.

"Dad, I just wish you would have told us. If you would have been honest about having a daughter for the beginning," says Christian.

"I don't hate you, dad, like Chris said. If you would have been honest, I at least would have understood," states Elijah.

"Me too" responds Levi.

"Me three", and "Same" follow by Mason and Ryder.

They understand.

They don't hate me.

I feel relieved that my boys don't hate me, and they accept why I kept Kyla from their knowledge.

"So, you all are all okay about Kyla?" I question them.

They all respond to me with a 'yes'.

"Does she know about us?" asks Christian. I shake my head as a no.

"You should probably tell her about us too, though" suggests Elijah. I nod as an answer.

"I will...Do you all want to be there?" I ask them, pleading that they be there for me and give me strength to tell her the truth too.

Before answering my question, they all look to each other. When they've decided they, face me, and Christian is the one to answer for them all.

"Sure, we will be there for you. And for her as well," says Christian. I give them a genuine smile as thanks.

I just hope it will go well when I tell Kyla the truth.

~

~

~

Author's Note: So how'd you think about this chapter? Now, they all finally know about Kyla! Writing this chapter was somewhat hard, to be honest.

Hope you enjoyed reading this chapter! :)

Chapter 7 - Sister

~ POV: Christian Bower ~

I have a little sister.

I remember growing up with my brothers, I always want a sister. I'm kind of excited to meet her, and she how she is. When I saw her earlier, she seemed uncomfortable, and a little upset. What could she upset about? Either way, I will be there for her now.

For whatever, it is she has me.

~~~

~ POV: Elijah Bower ~

Sister.

Wow. I would have never imagined having a sister. Nevertheless, a little sister. I wonder how her personality is like? Once dad was done telling us about Kyla, I had a flashback moment where I, kind of remembered that day that dad said when he took us all to the zoo. I'm sad that I don't remember her when she was small. It's nice that I know the truth about her.
~~~

I want to be an older brother to her, like I am with my brothers.

~~~

~ POV: Levi Bower ~

I was shocked when dad told us that Kyla was our little sister. Even though, she is only our half-sister, I don't care. Like the rest of two of brothers, who are also half-siblings, I don't care because to me they are my full siblings. I will see Kyla, as my little sister. Growing up, I would make scenarios in my mind where I'd pretend that had a sister. With that sister, I would look after her, take care of her, protect her, and love her.

I hope she doesn't react bad about us.

~~~

~ POV: Mason Bower ~

I still don't understand.

How? How could dad keep this from us?

Why keep the existence of your child from the rest of your children? How fucked up is that?

I don't hate my dad, I'm just a little hurt. She doesn't look like dad that much. I mean she has his lips, but besides that not much of a resemblance. She probably looks more like her mother. It doesn't matter to me. I don't care. I don't care about her. She's probably a spoiled brat, whose mother gives her everything she wants.

I don't want her in my way.

~~~

~ POV: Ryder Bower ~
~~~

Damn. This is so crazy.

We have a sister. A littler sister. I'm an older brother now.

When I'm at school, my teammates are all talking how they have to do pick up their sisters, look after them, and do all these other stuff for their sisters. I felt a little jealous of them, because it seemed that they really did care for their sisters. I know I have my brothers, but it's not the same. Now I can, do all different kinds of shit, an older brother and little sister do.

I'm excited to get to know her.

~~~

~ POV: Third-Person Narrative ~

Once Richard asked his sons, Christian, Elijah, Levi, Mason, and Ryder, if they wanted to be there when he tells Kyla the truth and that she has brothers, they all go to the room where Kyla went to. Before opening the door, Richard takes a deep breath as a way to help him ease his nerves. As Richards and the boys step into the room, they all think the same thing:

Here goes nothing.

~

~

~

Author's Note: Two chapter drops in one day?! I wanted to finally introduce the boys POV's, and though this would be a good way to introduce them. Feedback? I was thinking that for the next chapter(s), I could do one with Kyla's POV, and then one of her brother's or her father's POV. What do ya'll think?

Hope you enjoyed this chapter and have a good day! :)
~~~

Chapter 8 - Brothers

POV: Kyla Bower ~

I'm getting tired of waiting here.

What are they even doing?

Contemplating whether or not, I should just go to the main office where my dad and those boys or men, I hear multiple footsteps coming closer to the door of the room I'm in. The room I came in seem like sitting room; there was just comfortable chairs, two sofas facing each other, and a coffee table in the middle. I stand from where I'm seated when the door opens. The first to enter the room is my dad, then follows the boys.

Why do they keep being close to my dad's side?

"Kyla, I have to tell you something very important. Do you think you can let me talk, without interrupting me? I promise I'll answer any questions you have after, I just need to talk and explain things first, ok?" he rambles to me.

"Sure," I lie. "But why are they here if you're going to tell me something important?" I ask as I motion a hand to them.

"They're apart of what I'm going to tell you" he says. I nod in understanding, even though I'm so confused.

"Kyla, I'm sure you know where I was in the past twelve years. I was in prison, for something I didn't do. I need you to believe me when I say that it was the most hardest thing to do, when I had to leave you... and your brothers," he says slowly and softly.

Did I hear correctly? Brothers? That has to be wrong. I'm a single child.

"No. No, I don't have brothers. I'm a single child," I voice my thoughts to him. What the fuck is he saying? He's insane.

"You never knew this, but your mother did. I had children with other women with before having you. I wasn't married to them. We only had brief relationships, me and their mothers. But, with your mother is was different; I, we wanted to be together, get married. When I went I went to prison, I didn't know how long I'd be there. I didn't want her to wait for me. She didn't agree with me, but I didn't want to hold her back. Leaving her was hard for both of us."

"She knew I had kids, and she accepted that fact. I have five sons. When we were pregnant with you, it made us so, so happy. I couldn't wait for you to meet your brothers, and me. I was the happiest. You probably don't remember this, but when you were young I took you to the zoo; with five young boys, I told you they were my friend's kids. They weren't. They were my kids. I had to lie to their mothers and them to get you all to meet each other. I thought if you all met each other it's be easier when I told you the truth... I never got to tell you the truth," he tells me.

"But all of this is the truth. They are your brothers. We're together. We can be together finally," he ends as he takes a couple steps towards me. As he comes to me, I take steps back. I shake my head. This can't be true.

No, no, no.

My dad looks hurt as he sees me not wanting him to come close to me. Then, the boys that were near my father's side try coming to me, too. "No," I say sternly looking at them; I still can't believe this, I just can't.

"Kyla, baby, I -" my dad starts but before he can sat anything further I cut him off. "No. I'm not your daughter. You're just someone who I just met" I shout, not even wanting to shout. He looks hurt, but quickly composes himself not wanting me to see him that way. The boys looks back and forth from him to me.

Hurt that I didn't know the truth, I feel suffocated being enclosed in the same space as my dad and "brothers". Keeping my eyes on my dad, then glancing at the boys every once in a while, I stumble back making my way out the room. Thinking that they wouldn't see me moving backwards, I accidentally hit my side with a chair, almost falling. Christian tries to help me stable myself. "Don't come close to me" I tell him. Christian looks at me taken aback and sad.

I can't deal with this right now. It's too much.

I manage to get out the room, but look back at them one last time. They look at me with a mix of emotions but mostly sadness and concern.

I need away from them.

~~~

~ POV: Bower boys (Christian, Elijah, Levi, Mason, and Ryder) ~

That went well. Ha. That went to shit.

We won't give up on her. She will just have to get to use to us. We're her brothers.

~~~

~ POV: Richard Bower ~

Shit.

That went horribly wrong, then I expected. I didn't think that she's have that reaction of betrayal, hurt, and anger in eyes. I had thought that she'd be mad and disappointed in me, after all; I was so wrong. Honestly, I don't know how I thought she'd react. I haven't seen her since was 4, twelve years ago. Twelve years.

I want Kyla to not regret me. I want my daughter to have a relationship with me, as father-daughter. I don't want her to push me away. I need to speak with Mary, her mother, to discuss having Kyla spend sometime with me. I want her to at least get to know her brothers.

I feel like an asshole. She it's so hard to describe how she felt from looking into her eyes as I told her. The one emotion I saw vividly in her eyes, was betrayed.

When she went backwards as I tried going to her, I was like a cut was going through my chest. My heart.

I just want my baby.

I know she's not a little girl anymore, she's a young women. But to me she's my baby that I never saw growing up.

~

~

~

Author's Note: Kyla knows the truth now! Let's see where it goes from here for the Bower family...

Hope you enjoyed the chapter, til next time :)

Chapter 9 – Away from these people

Just as Kyla, had ran from the room she was closed in with her father and now, brothers. She got in a room that the butler, or guy that had lead them to the main office, had told her was her room. Her own room. She had not had her own room, since she living with her mother and grandmother when they were alive.

Kyla had plopped herself on her bed. The room was decorated so beautifully, had natural lighting shining through the windows, and an amazing bathroom, along with a nice organized closest. As she laid on her bed, she stared at her ceiling.

So many things ran on and on in her head like: Why tell me now? Did he ever think of me? my opinion? Why didn't my "brothers" ever reach out to me? along with other things. Still, all of Kyla's questions led her to think of a reason why. She could not wrap her brain around it. She felt like she was the little kid that was invited last minute to a birthday party, where they never wanted to be invited in the first place. Kyla felt like she was left in the dark, and mad.

Being in this house, this mansion, with her father and her now brothers, she felt so small. Lost. She wanted to be alone, away from these people who thought themselves as her family. Kyla knew they were blood related, but did not see them as family. She did not think of them as family, and she did not know if she would ever think of them that way.

I need out. Out of this house. Away from these people, Kyla thought.

The idea of getting away from the mansion became appealing. The more she went over it in her head, the more and more of a good ideas it sounded to her. Suddenly, she sat up straight in her bed and went to the closet where her got a nice bag and filled it with some clothing pieces. She packed underclothes, one pair of sweat pants and jeans, two shirts, and one oversized tee shirt; along with some essentials.

Slowly, Kyla made her way down the stairs, not wanting to cause any noise to alert anyone in the house. Somehow, she had made her way into the garage where she saw many cars, nice cars. She grabbed the first pair of keys her hand caught. When she found the car, that the keys belonged to she settled in, and soon enough the car was ignited to life.

Not having any place in mind, she had made her direction to Downtown Los Angeles. Growing up, Kyla had visited Los Angeles plenty of times. She had went on roadtrips with her mom and grandma to Los Callejones, Anaheim to go to amusement parks, and other interesting places. Once she was in the city, Kyla decided to just drive around for a while.

Tried of driving, she decided to go to motel to spend the night. Finding the nearest motel, she went to the office securing her room she go her bag from the car to her room. When she was away from the mansion, she had discarded her phone all together. Pulling out her phone, she let a loud sigh out. She had 40 missed call from unknown numbers, and a shit ton of messages from the same unknown numbers who she presume was from her dad and the boys. Wanting to avoid their lectures, she powered off her phone and laid in the bed.

On the last note before drifting off sleep, all she wanted was for this awful day to end.

~~~

Meanwhile at the mansion, Richard, Christian, Elijah, Levi, Mason, and Ryder were very concerned for the younger Bower member. Since going to check up on Kyla, Ryder, saw her room empty and went on the search to look for his sister. When Ryder was out of luck, he ran downstairs to the living room telling everyone Kyla was not in the mansion.

"What do you mean she's not here?" asked Richard quickly becoming concerned.

"I went to her room to go talk to her and she wasn't there" said Ryder.

"We'll go look for her outside" announced Elijah and Levi.

"I'll go look her her in the other rooms" Ryder said.

"Me too," blurted Mason.

"Dad and me will check out front" decides Christian.

With no luck, on finding Kyla anywhere in or outside the mansion, they were all scare of the thought of what could have happened to her. A lightbulb idea, went off in Christian's mind:

"We should track her phone."

Richard pulling out his phone quickly and handing it to his oldest son, Christian went on to looking for her location. Within seconds, they all saw
~~~

her location was in Downtown Los Angeles. Looking for the location, on maps they found that her location was in a sketchy motel.

Without a doubt, Richard snatched his phone from his oldest sons' hand and ran to the garage to get in a car. Not even caring if his sons were following him, he pressed on the gas to go get his daughter. Following their father, to go get their little sister they all slid into the a large car.

All the men hoped that Kyla was safe.

~~~

Bolting from the car, Ricard ran to the office of the motel, with his sons arriving shortly after him. The motel looked small, sketchy, and rundown. How could she think of just coming here, by herself, he thought. When inside the office, Richard along with his sons who stood behind him, waited impatiently for the person in the front desk to come to front. They were all waiting while pressing the call bell, when a short women came from the back; the women just stared at the men in front of her, annoyed that they had interrupted her midway into her scratcher.

"Is there a Kyla Bower staying in this motel? In what room number?" questioned Richard terrified of worse that could happen to his daughter.

"Can't give ya that information" the women responded with while inspecting her red painted nails.

"Do you know that you have a minor staying at this motel, without an adult by her side?" Richard seethed. Feeling irritated with the women, Richard was starting to flex his hands into fists; trying to somehow relief his angry with the women. Not wanting any trouble at almost midnight, the women told them the room number that Kyla was staying in. Hearing the room number, all the men sprinted in search of the room. The first to make it to the room was Mason, where he began to pound on the door with both his fists.
~~~

Waking up, scared from her sleep at the pounding on the door, Kyla went to the door infuriated with whoever was on the other side of the door. Not even thinking who was at the door, she unlocked it and came to sight with who she least expected.

"What the hell?" Kyla ruffed out still tired.

"'What the hell?' Really? What the hell are you doing here, Kyla? Hm?" let out Richard. As he waited for her response, he took a chance at scanning her body to make sure she was not hurt. He felt like a bit of weight was lifted off his shoulders as he saw that she was okay.

"I was sleeping. Clearly, you don't care that you woke me up" she mumbled the last part to her self, but more angrily referring to her dad and the boys.

"We don't care? Really, that's what you think?" Levi shouted a little.

"I didn't ask you all to come get me did I, now?" Kyla also shouted back.

"You didn't have to! We were worried!" retorted Elijah.

"Again. I. Did. Not. Ask. For. That. To" she spat back, glaring at all the men.

"Enough! We're going back to the mansion, get you things Kyla" Richard tiredly said, as he ran a hand down his face.

"No," said Kyla confidently.

"Kyla. Get you things now!" yelled Richard to her. He said that with no room for discussion. Kyla flinched back at the sound of her father yelling at her, knowing that there was not other option that to listen she meekly got her bag and went out the room with them. Ryder went to the office of the motel to pay for it, after making his way to the car.

With everyone situated into they had came in, Kyla followed her father. Buckled into the car, they drove back to the mansion. The tension in the car was thick. Not a word was said between, either Richard or Kyla; in the other car with all the boys, it remained quiet, not a word was spoken from anyone.

~

~

~

Author's Note: Hey everyone! Hope ya'll are having a good start to the week. This week I'm starting , my new job but I'll still be posting so don't worry! Comment on how you thought this chapter was with the third person POV.

Hope you enjoyed this chapter :)

Chapter 10 - Permission

Arriving at the house, I didn't even realize that I had fallen asleep during the car ride back to the mansion. My dad and I did not speak to each other the during the whole drive. The tension was thick in the car, it was getting stuffy. Right when the car was put in park, I made a run for the door of the garage to the house. I still wanted to be alone, away from them. Already up the stairs, my dad yells my name, making me jump from fear.

Who the hell does he think, he's yelling at?

Slowly making my way downstairs from the top of the stairs, I see my father standing near the front doors with all the boys a little to his right side. I am not looking forward to this little lecture that he wants to go into.

"What can I do for you, Richard?" I say to him with a fake smile.

"First, I want respect from you, then, I want you to tell me why you were at a motel? Might I add without my permission," he says back to me putting all his attention on me. I return my attention to him too, but I also catch a glimpse of some of the boys shifting on their feet, while Christian is the only one standing straight. He is the only one actively focusing on the conversation between my father and I.

"And why should I do that? Uhm? I don't see the reason why I should be telling you anything" I say as I take a step toward him.

"I'm you father that's wh-"

"But are you really? My father? You were never in my life to begin with," I cut in as he's talking. My dad's eyes widen as he takes in my words, but plays it off as if nothing. He didn't expect me to say that, but I could honestly care less of what he thinks. "You know why I couldn't be in your life, even if I could back then I want to make it up to you and be in it now," he tells me directly.

"Well, it's a little too late for that don't you think? If it's any consolation, at least you were able to be in their lives" I nod in the direction of my dad's sons'. "I plan to be in your life, Kyla; whether you or your mother like it or not" he said.

At the mention of my mom, my heart clenches. I want her to be with me so badly. But she will never be able to be in it anymore.

"I don't want you in it my life. So. Stay. Out. Of. It!" I slowly enunciate to him as if it'll set in his head.

"Enough! Enough of this, Kyla. This ends here. Go back to your room" He defeatedly says.

"No," I simply say. "No, I won't go bac-" I start to add, but get quickly interrupted by my dad.

"Kyla, go to your room!" he shouts at me. At the tone of his voice, I jump from being caught off guard. At my action, his eyes soften slightly. Reluctantly, I go back to my room from earlier; there's not much I can do now, and with my dad looking at me, I can't really do anything besides listen to him. Midway through the stairs, my dad announces that there are still things to be discussed tomorrow. I stop my steps, wanting to turn around and make eye contact but I stop myself. Once closed inside my room, I plop myself on the bed getting myself in the covers. Lying in bed, I will for sleep to come at me, but nothing. I go over everything that was said moments ago.

This whole situation is shit, I think before closing my eyes to the abyss of sleep.

~~~

The next morning, I wake up and notice that it is dark outside. My skin is covered with a slick of sweat; I can feel the sweat beads on my forehead starting to make their way down to the side of my face. I was awoken by the nightmare of how my mom and grandma died. Only in my dream, I am the only one left in the car going staring towards the mountain cliffs without being able to move. In my dream, I try everything to free myself from the car to get out, but never succeed. I never know in my dream, if I die. Every time I have that nightmare, something different happens like, just as I am getting to free myself the car hit the cliff, or my mom and grandma are with me in car. Fuck, I just wanted to sleep. I don't want to get up, but I know that I won't be going back to sleep.

Getting out of bed, I decide to take a shower. In the bathroom, take a look at myself in the mirror and the first thing I notice is how much of a mess I look like and cringe. My naturally wavy hair is all over my head, I have dark circles under my eyes, and I still have the clothes on from yesterday that I never took off. Having see how bad I look like, I strip my clothes off and plummet myself under the hot, steaming water of the shower. I let myself drown in the feeling the water cascading over me. It feels nice.
~~~

After finished with my shower, I get ready to change into some black leggings, a brown long sleeve and my faded black and white vans. Once having a mental battle of whether to go downstairs to see the house or not, I go with the first option; Slowly tip-toeing down, I get to the bottom of the stairs wanting to go out to the backyard and walk around, when I suddenly sense an other presence coming from somewhere. I go to look to see who is possibly awake at this early in the morning, as I enter the kitchen and see that there is Christian, Levi, and my dad seated on the kitchen island. They haven't noticed that I'm in the kitchen, but I see that they all look tired. Levi gets out of his spot and goes to the coffee machine; that's when I guess Levi feels me observing them and turns his head my way.

Having been discovered awake, I stay where I am near the entrance of the kitchen. I don't know what to do. Thinking it's better to leave the kitchen, Levi then calls me and motions for me to come closer to them to take a seat. I don't want to sit next to my dad or Christian, so I come up with the only thing on my mind.

"I actually have to use the restroom now, so..." I say walking backwards before they say anything, and bolt from the kitchen to my room. In the safety of my room, I lock myself inside and exhale a long breath. With my back on my bedroom door, I slide to the floor with my knees to my chest and settle my head on my knees. This is going to be one interesting morning.

~

~

~

A/N: Hi! Sorry for not having posted, been very, very busy with school and homework. Anyways...

Hope you enjoyed reading this chapter, til next time :)

Chapter 11 - Terms I

~ POV: Richard Bower ~

As Kyla ran up the stairs, I watched as she left without another word. I know for a fact that she is not use to the idea of the boys or me being with her. I would want her to spend time with us, to just be with us without wanting to run from our very presence.

I will have to make sure she knows I am here for her. That I am not going away from her this time.

She'll have to get use to having us, as part of her family.

~~~

~ POV: Levi Bower ~

Kyla, sure doesn't want us around her. I don't even know how or when I would approach her. She seems so closed off from people. Is she normally like with the people she's comfortable with? With her mom? I might not know much about her, but I'd at least like to get to know her; or for her to know me.

But where do I even start?
~~~

~~~

~ POV: Christian Bower ~

I don't know if Kyla is just acting rebellious to dad, or she's just having a hard time getting use to the idea of us in her life. I know it must be hard. But we have to make this work in order to be able to be a family one day; it has to work. Where even was Kyla in the past 12 years?

I need to find more information about her, so that day or anyone won't get hurt.

~~~

~ POV: Kyla Bower ~

A sudden knock on the door, awake me from where I'm seated from the door. I didn't even realize that I fell asleep on the floor. My body must have been very tired, yet I only feel like I am mentally and emotionally drained. I stand to open the door, and find Ryder on the other side.

"Can I help you?" I ask warily, looking him up and down.

"Dad wants us to all to have breakfast together in the dining room. I came to come get you, since I thought you probably don't know where it was. So... yeah" he tells me as he's done rambling.

"Oh. Um... sure. Give me a sec" I tell him as I go to put on a pair of shoes. Closing my bedroom door behind me, I follow Ryder has he walks in front of me. Going down the stairs with Ryder, I being to feel my heartbeat rise a little in my ears. I don't get why I'm a getting anxious out of nowhere. I shouldn't care about them. Rounding the dining room, I stop in my tracks; getting takeover by my growing anxiety. Ryder must have sensed that I stoped because he turned to face me with his face tilted to the side, looking at me with curiousness.

"Why are stopping? Come on, we're all hungry," he tells me as he grabs my wrist and drags me with him.

As Ryder goes to sit with his brothers and dad, I stare at them quietly not knowing where or what to do. There are only two seats: one to the side of dad and another next to Elijah. Without anyones' acknowledgment, I make a beeline to the seat next to Elijah but not before stealing a glance at dad before; he had a hint of hurt in his eyes and tried to cover it up. thinking no one would see.

Sitting at the table with them, I don't know what to do with myself. I see as Ryder begins to fill his plate with food, Mason continuing to eat his, while both Levi and Elijah are engrossed in a conversation amongst them, as is Christian and dad. Not trying to seem so obvious that I'm looking at them, yet failing, Levi and I make eye contact for a brief seconds. Quickly, I advert my eyes and go to set food on my plate. I get some fruit, eggs, and toast.

As I go to. take a bite from my plate, I hear grunt come from across from me to see that it came from Mason. I look up at him, for him to then roll his eyes at me. I did.t do anything to hime for him to be rolling his eyes at me. Ryder must have seen Mason's action towards me because he elbows him on the side, receiving an "ow" from Mason. Not feeling hungry anymore, I just move the food on my plate mindlessly.

"You should eat something" Elijah whispers in my ear.

Still looking at my plate moving the food around, Ryder then says, "It's not good to have an empty stomach" and I see Levi nod silently. Somehow dad must have hear Ruder, since from the head of the table he sternly says to me directly, "Kyla, please eat something".

"I'm not really hungry" I mumble as an answer. "Well, you have to at least try" dad says once more.

"What are we even doing? " I utter as everyone seems to want to address my eating habits.

"Ok. Fine, if that's what you want" dad speaks to me with sarcasm. "You went out without anyone knowing, or with permission, Kyla. You went alone to a motel, when you could have stayed here; at home with your family. Still, I get that the news of grandma must have affected you in some way, so your not punish. At least not this time, but don't do that again. I just what to know why you went out by yourself? Why?" he continues.

"I just didn't want to with any of you. I wanted to be alone" I state honestly. "With that being said, I better get going. It was good meeting you all I suppose, or well again I guess, but this little family reunion is done for me," I voice as I motion to the everyone at the table as I stand.

"And where do you think you're doing?" Christian asks me.

"I'm going home, to my house" I answer him with confidence.

"This is your home, Kyla. With your family" dad adds.

"No. This isn't home, I don't even know you guys. You're just people I barely met" I say getting irritated.

"We are your family. Your brothers and me, as your father"

"No, because from what I'm getting out of this whole situation is that your just people in my way" I retort back to my dad firmly.

"Whether, you like it or not we're you family now" Elijah says nonchalantly.

"Well, I'm leaving. So you all can figure out what you're all going to do" I finish as I go to walk out of the dining room.

"What about the inheritance?" Levi questions. "I don't know, but I going" I answer him back. "Have you forgotten the terms? It's that we all live together or it nothing for anyone" he quickly says.

Shit. I forgot about the stupid terms. I attempt to recall Mr. Haydes words:

"You all must live together for a year in this estate."

~

~

~

A/N: Hello! How's it going everyone? Issue will be addresses next chapter ... so who will be hurt then? On another note, who's your favorite character so far? let know if you have any suggestions or who's POV you'd like to see next? Till next time!

Hope you enjoyed reading this chapter :)

Chapter 12 - Terms II

~ POV: Third Person~

"You all must live together for a year in this estate."

~

After recalling Mr. Haydes words, Kyla shakes her head slightly as if it would help vanish the words that had ran through her head seconds ago. To herself she swears, Levi brought up the terms of the inheritance now out of all times, to prevent her from leaving. And he got me too, Kyla thinks to herself.

Turing to look at them, Kyla sees in their eyes that they won't let her go easily. It makes Kyla wonder their actual motives. Do they only want me to say for the money or as part of a family? Raising an eyebrow skeptically as an indication that she's listening, as she goes to return to her seat from the dining table.

"The terms clearly stated that it's that we all live together for a year here or absolutely no one gets anything" rephrases Levi again, seeing as has he has a glint of victory in his eyes that he managed to get Kyla with them for a moment. "I know" Kyla mumbles to them as she looks down at her lap. In her mind Kyla, does not want to spend an entire year with them. She'd rather get stuck with anyone else but them; she'd even go with her aunt and cousins, although they'd willingly take her in, she knew they probably would be hesitant too since they have to fed another mouth and take care of her. They had helped her out in the beginning after the death of her grandma and mom, but had changed a little towards her. Kyla had dismissed their change, as a way of coping. She planned to pay them back one way in the future. Maybe I can pay them back with my part of the inheritance? she thought to herself.

Kyla needed that money. She wanted to become someone in this life. She wanted a career, yet still didn't know in what, good paying check, and a place to call home instead of barely making ends meet. Yes, she had worked with Gina in the diner, but no one knew that she was motherless, or alone. She wasn't going to tell anyone of these men that her mother had died, especially her dad.

Kyla stayed quiet in her seat as everyone stared at her. They had no idea what ran through her head, all they wanted was for her to stay. Well, everyone besides Mason; he didn't want her with them. He thought that in the short time they had known her again she managed to make them worry and scared shitless for her, and she seemed ungrateful. Meanwhile, Kyla knew want she had to do, even if she did't want this to happen so she declared:

"I'll stay" she said ever so quietly thinking no one had heard her but they somehow had heard her words. A little shocked that she had willingly agreed to stay with them, and not put a fight, Richard was taken aback. Regardless, Richard was happy to have his baby with him. Relief went through Christian, Elijah, Levi and Ryder's bodies. They wanted their sister to the with them. A wave of anger and a little happiness ran through him.

Clearing his throat and recomposing himself Richard said, "Good, but we can't forget what you did last night. So I believe that rules have to be placed". Kyla rolled her eyes at the mention of rules. She had managed to look out for herself, without anyone's help; but she thought she'd go along with them. For now at least. If there was a rules that she didn't agree with, she wouldn't follow it. "Fine. Go ahead and do tell the so-called rules" she put emphasis on the last word as she told them.

"1. You respects your brothers and me. Respect goes both ways.

2. You ask and let us know if you're going out. Always tell one of your brothers if I'm not here, but tell me.

3. No drinking or smoking.

4. No boys.

5. Lights out at 11 pm on weekdays, and 12 am on weekends. No later than that unless necessary.

Got it?" Richard spoke to Kyla directly as he slightly narrowed his eyes.

"Crystal... But now you must do something for me too, Richard, in order for me to follow your rules," Kyla told her father. With a small nod, as an indication to proceed Richard was ready to hear what Kyla had to say. "I do not want you to contact or get in touch in anyway space of form to my mother. She's happy now, and I don't want you, messing that up for her just because you want her back. If you need to talk to my mom, for whatever reason you tell me. You didn't want her in your life at one point, well guess what? I don't want you in her's either. Got it?" Kyla had said with such disdain to Richard.

Richard didn't want to agree with his daughters rule, still deep down he knew she was right. If her mom, Mary, was happy he could take that away from her. So nonetheless it was why he reluctantly said, "I understand".

Out of now where, Elijah stepped forth to Kyla. He felt that Kyla was going to make everything in her power to avoid his brothers and him. He was not wrong, Kyla didn't plan anytime soon to play siblings with them. "We also ask that you follow something from us" he noted turning to his brothers to seek their approval. With a silent approval between them all, he continued, "you must spend time with us everyday for at least an hour." In her ear he whispered, "because if not we can make your time her unbearable".

Kyla was not scared of the boys. Yet, after hearing Elijah's words, she grew a little terrified at the idea of them doing anything to her. His words sounded as a warning, instead of a threat.

"Okay, then" she answered them calmly, although she was still wary and wasn't going to open up to them in the ear future. "I guess these are the terms for us, if we're going to make it work for a year"

"I'm going to head up to my room now" Kyla let them know not even asking them if she could, not leaving any room for discussion. Once in her room, Kyla let out a breathe she didn't;t know she was holding. While downstairs her anxiety was skyrocketing. She was trying her hardest to not let them see how anxious she was or would have had an anxiety attack.

All I have to do is follow there terms for a year with them, Kyla repeated to herself as a mantra.

~

~

~

Hope you liked this chapter :)

Chapter 13 - Sobrina

~ POV: Mason Bower ~

As Kyla leaves the dining room, more like runs from from us, dad and my brothers stay quiet. This whole situation with Kyla is stupid. I'm not saying Kyla, herself, is stupid, but they way everything is going about is. She's probably an attention seeker for dad. And those rules she demanded dad? How could she even ask him to do that? Dad doesn't know a single thing to know about Kyla. He has to be in contact with her mother. I kinda of remember meeting Mary, but not too much. I remember she was nice, and treated all of us like if we were her kids. That's all in the past though, it can't be changed.

"So you're actually going to do what she's telling you?'" I questioned dad in a hard tone. I didn't mean for my question to be delivered that way, but it's not like I can do anything about it. I watched as dad let out a frustrated sigh and ran a hand down his face.

"I intend to," he says. At hearing his words, I felt a surge of rage go through me. How can he even listen to something like that, that a little girl said? He's going to be hurting. I know for a fact by justing looking at dad, whenever Mary is mentioned how his expression softens and his eyes hold longing, that he missed her. Loves her.

Dad was never like that with any of our mothers. Christian, Elijah, Levi have the same mother, Lorna; Ryder and me have the same mother. Our mothers' get along, they're basically best friends. I admit that at the beginning they didn't like each other, but they shared a few things: Children from the same father, and their dislike for dad. If they would have known of Mary and Kyla, they would've went ballistic; they would've tried to make their lives' miserable and done anything to get them away from dad.

"How can you even consider listening to her? She's just a little girl who only wants attention. How can't you see that?" I angrily ask dad, narrowing my gaze to him.

"Just drop it, Mason," Ryder grumbles next to me. Choosing to ignore him, I keep going on.

"No. You haven't seen her in twelve fucking years! Twelve! She doesn't want to be with you, can't you see that? You should've just her leav-" I rant, but am interrupted by dad shouting back at me.

"Mason, shut it! I don't care what you think. She's my child! Just like the rest of you are. If you're done with your rant, stop act acting like a child," he finishes. He gets up from his seat at the head of the table and leaves the dinning room. The table still remains quiet, but only for a couple minutes.

"Why would you say to dad?" Levi ask directly for me.

Staying quiet, I storm out of the room. If they can't see that I'm only looking out for them, then that's on them. I go to my room, but before that I hear talking coming from Kyla's room. She's talking in a hush tone. I head to her door, and put my hear to her door to hear what is being said.

~ POV: Kyla Bower ~

In the safety of my room, I try to calm myself down before getting an anxiety attack. The talk downstairs was a hell. All I wanted was for it to be over. Having their eyes on was uncomfortable; I go hid somewhere, where they couldn't see me.

After a few minutes, I managed to calm myself down. Going to my bed to lay down, my phone starts to ring. Going to my phone, I see that the caller ID indicate that it's my aunt Elena. my mother only had one sister, who has three kids: Guadalupe, Manuel, and Maricella. When I was younger, my cousin's and I use to get along really well; then out of nowhere, we didn't. They grew jealous of me for some reason. I don't even know why she's calling me, but nevertheless I answer her call.

"Yes, tia?" I answer with an annoyed voice.

"Ay, y ese tono? Que no sabes saludar a tu única tia? La que te a ayudado?" She asks in Spanish with a mocking tone.[Translation: Ay, and that tone? You don't know how to greet your only aunt? The one that's helped you?]

Rolling my eyes, to no one in particular I play go along with her. "Perdon tia. To how do I owe the pleasure of this phone call, you have generously bestowed me?" I say full with sarcasm.

"You hear me good, chamaca [girl]. Don't talk to my like, porque vas a ver [because you'll see]. Te advierto [I warn you]. You know that you owe me money, when will I get it?" she says in a low voice, which to her means business.

"You'll get it, I just sometime. Te voy a mandar ahora, no me apuras [I'll send you right now, don't rush me]".

"The bills don't wait for you, sobrina" she says was she hangs up on me.

My aunt Elena was the only one that helped me when my mom and grandma died. She lent me the money to be able to bury them, even though it was her mother too that died. She didn't give a fuck. Ever since I borrowed money from her, she holds it over my head every time. Frustrated, I throw my phone across the room; making it crack even more than it already is. Closing my eyes, I try to hold back my tears of frustration. I'm so done with her. I stand from my bed, and decide to go out and explore the estate.

As I'm leaving my room and walking with my head down lost in thought, I collide with a wall that I didn't even know was there. Recovering from the collide, I realize that the wall, was Mason. Oh, goody.

"Who were you on the phone with?" he questions without missing a chance.

"It's none of your business"

"Who was it?" he say exasperated.

"No one"

Quickly he steps toward me. I go back with every step he takes, not liking how angry he looks. My back hits a wall and he traps me. "I'm going to ask you for the last time. Who was on with phone with you?" The way that Mason is acting scares the shit out of me. But not trying to look intimidated, I retort, "It was no one important," as I use all my strength to push him off me.

I run from him not taking a chance to look behind. I decide to start exploring the estate outside, away from Mason, the boys, and dad. They don't have to know how much they terrify me.

~

~

~

Hope you liked this chapter :)

Chapter 14 - Around

~ POV: Third Person ~

As Kyla went outside to explore the estate, she went around the back of the house where she first saw a pool. Without seeing first, if there was anyone at the pool she made her way there; approaching the pool she looked at the water which was clear, pristine blue. She bended down to her knees and proceeded to touch the water. She liked the way it felt to her touch, how the water would ripple just from a touch of her finger. Oh, how she wished that her life was as still as untouched water, she thought. But no life had other plans.

She hadn't heard when the doors that led to the backyard opened, until two sets of feet appeared in her line of vision. Looking up to see the owners of said feet, she saw that it was Elijah and and Ryder looking down at her with curious eyes. Kyla had sensed that Elijah was reserved and the most quiet from among the brothers. He didn't talk much unless talked to first, or if he felt the need to talk, but he seemed very astute. On the other hand, Ryder, although the youngest of brothers gave off the vibe of not having a care in the world. He seemed friendly, and was fun talking too, but when he cared about something he cared passionately like being apart of his band that he had mentioned.

Turning slightly so that they don't see her roll her eyes she asked them, "What do you want?"

"Nothing. We came outside for a swim since it's been awhile since we've been here," Ryder answered her happily with a grin on his face."Mm, good for you then," Kyla told them with a dry laugh as she got up. Once up, Kyla, turned to leave and continue her venture of the estate; Yet not before Elijah added, "Would you like to join us?"

Debating whether nor not, to join them she was having difficulty an internal conflict with herself. She couldn't allow them to get close to her. She tried to remind herself that her only family, her mom and grandma had died, and she had none left. So with that in mind Kyla said, "No. I'm good thanks though," and she brushed her hands together. She saw the hurt on both their faces, but shrugged it off, and trying not to cared about it too much or else she knew she would cave in. She only got a few steps before Elijah said something to her.

"We'd like it if you joined us. We're going to be living together, so there will be times where we have to interact together; so join us, it'll be fun." Kyla didn't know what to say to him because he was right. She thought back to her earlier thoughts. "I can't. I'm a little busy now," she made-up quickly which was half-true. Not looking back at them she went on with looking around the house.

~

Kyla had seen everything she thought was possible to see in the estate. From the garden with plants and flowers, to the pool, to the library (which she loved), the offices, art room (which she took a liking too), and more endless rooms. She was about to head back to her room to rest, from all the walking she had done when she stumbled upon the music room. In inside the music room, it was huge; there were an assortment of different instruments from guitars, violins, drums, to many more. Yet, what caught Kyla's eyes was the grand piano that was positioned at one corner of the room near one of the many long windows. It's beautiful she thought. She went to the piano letting her fingers brush the keys.

She couldn't hold back from sitting down on the bench of the marvelous instrument. She sat down as she admired the instrument that was glossy black, and dust-free. She decided to put the fine instrument to her use since no one was there to bother her.

Kyla had been told from her music teacher from her high school in the past that it was as if music was able to flow naturally from her; She didn't believe them. She did not have that much training like others did. Kyla had taught herself how to play with a piano that was in her old house before her mother had to sell it to make a little money out of it to pay off bills, when she was alive.

(A/N: I advise that if your reading this part to play the song from the top at the same time after the end of this paragraph)Playing with the keys, she then settled with playing a song that she thought fit with how she was feeling inside: Camden by Gracie Abrams; the meaning she got from the song was that overthinking or intrusive thoughts don't leave but stay haunting the mind. Kyla let the music flow from her fingers to the keys, it was as if the music has possessed her too, and she began to sing along with the tune of the piano.

Self diagnosing 'til I'm borderlineI'll do whatever helps to sleep at night-Until I'm feeling like an islandUntil I'm strong enough to hide itWhat was I thinking looking for a sign?As if I've ever seen the stars alignSomebody take over the drive andSomebody notice how I'm tryingSomebody notice how I'm trying

As a child, Kyla always found the piano to be a wonderful instrument that felt calming to the ear which drew her to it.

I never said it, but I know that II bury baggage 'til it's out of sightI think it's better if I hide itI really hope that I survive this

When done playing, Kyla felt slightly out of breathe but also... relief? Somehow she knew that she would be fine, one way or another, from this whole situation with her dad and the boys. Closing her eyes and draping her head to her folded arms that leaned on the piano, she hadn't noticed when anyone had entered the room until someone was clapping their hands; she jumped from her seat on the bench a little frightened from the whoever was clapping til she turned around and saw it was the boy that had opened the door for her when she first came with Mr. Haydes and had shown them to the office where she had seen her dad again; but she didn't know his name.

"Sorry, I didn't mean to scare you. Didn't know you knew how to play?" the boy said as he pointed to the piano with a small smile. His voice was deep and a little husky; she liked the sound of it.

"No, you're good, just didn't know I had an audience looking" she responded returning a small smile to him.

"You're really good by the way. What song were you sing too?"

"You probably don't know her but it was by Gracie Abrams."

"Yeah, haven't heard of her. Sorry-"

"Oh, don't be. It's not everyones cup of tea" she said happily to him. "What's your name? I don't think I ever got it."

"Leo" he answered her as he extended a hand to which he took.

"Kyla, but you probably knew it," she mumbled back to him.

"I should let you know that, the food will be ready in an hour if you were going out of here. But your brothers, will have called for you or looked for you. Didn't think you'd like that very much," he said as he scratched the back of his head and looked down.

"Thanks, was going to leave anyways too" she told him as she went to the door of the music room to go find her room. "Bye" she said as she waved Leo, goodbye too.

~

~

~

Author's Note: This chapter was so fun to write about! I do not play the piano whatsoever, but when I was small I had a piano at some point in my life; But sadly my mom and I had to sell it because we were moving houses. Anywho... what did you all think about this chapter? Thoughts on Leo? or Kyla until now? Well, till next time...

Hope you liked this chapter :)

Chapter 15 - Changed Entirely

~ POV: Leo Martin ~

When mom first told me that Mrs. Isabel's family was going to be coming to stay in the estate, I didn't think too much about it; or rather anything at all. That is until Kyla came. I didn't even know that Mrs. Isabel had a granddaughter, all I knew was that she had five grandson's who were doing well. However, from what I've been told by my parents is that the whole Bower family, had changed when Mr. Richard went to prison.

The whole atmosphere of the house too, had changed entirely. The house had turned bleak and dull.

My parents have worked for the Bower's my whole life. The Bower boys and me grew up together along with my older brother, Alexander. We're all family; I consider them my brothers too. Ryder and me are the closed in age and get along better than the rest; I was five years old when everything changed and went to shit. Anyways, the point is that now with Mrs. Isabel dead, Mr. Richard out of prison, and a new addition to the Bower family, everything is changing too quickly. But I think it's all for the better; I hope so.

~

Walking into the kitchen, I smelt the wonderful aroma of my mom's cooking. Her food is the best, yet she doesn't believe it from my dad, me, or the Bower's; She doesn't like the attention. Still, arriving at the kitchen I notice how much food mom made, it looked like a feast instead of dinner.

"What's with all the food, mom?" I ask her as her back is facing me. She jumps a little from being startled from my sudden presence.

"Oh my! You scared me! And all the food is for dinner"

"It's a bit much isn't it for dinner" I say as I lift an eyebrow.

"Now that I'm looking at it... Yes, but it's just that I want to Kyla like it here, and if my cooking does the trick then so be it! Plus, I want to leave a good impression with her," she answered me in an anxious yet excited voice. Mom is always trying to make good impressions with people with her food, so this isn't anything too unusual. Her food is the best.

The only thing that's unusual in the estate is Kyla, I think to myself. When I saw her at first, she looked like any teenage girl, I didn't think anything too special about her. Yet, when she gave me a small smile as a thanks when showing Mr. Haydes and her, to the office it had not reached her eyes. Seeing that on her face, I won't lie it intrigued me. Seeing as how she hid her emotions, but I caught onto them just from staring into her eyes; her eyes captivated me.

"I'll be back mom. I'm just going to go back to my room for a bit till dinner. At 7 pm, right?" I question leaving the kitchen sticking my head from the side of the door, to still see my mom's respond.

"Hmm. Like always, Leo; you should know this be now," she tells me with a sarcastic hint in her tone.

Leaving the kitchen, I see all the Bower boys' and Richard all in the living room. They're all there together talking; they seem to be having a good time talking to one another, unless their good at acting they they do. Mason is talking with Elijah, Richard to Ryder, and Levi with Christian. But the only one that's missing is Kyla. I had seen her before walking outside, I had thought that she wanted some fresh air. I should go and get her.

After looking for Kyla outside and most of the rooms inside of the house, I still go on to look for her. I'm about to go and see if she's been in her room after all, until I hear something. Trying to follow the noise, it leads me to the music room. Could it be Kyla? I think. Pressing my ear to the door of the music room, I hear the sound of the piano being played. She must have been fiddling with the piano's keys because she settles on playing a song; a couple minutes pass and I hear singing coming from the other side.

I don't want to eavesdrop but I already did it; so going inside and watching her play wouldn't hurt anyone. Right? Either way I open the door and step inside, trying not wanting to scare her in case she stops playing.

Self diagnosing 'til I'm borderlineI'll do whatever helps to sleep at night-Until I'm feeling like an islandUntil I'm strong enough to hide itWhat was I thinking looking for a sign?As if I've ever seen the stars alignSomebody take over the drive andSomebody notice how I'm tryingSomebody notice how I'm trying

Hearing her sing is something else. Something entrancing and I can't seem to take my eyes off her, as she play. I don't know what the song is she is singing, but the way she sings the song it like she's putting all her emotions into the song.

I never said it, but I know that II bury baggage 'til it's out of sightI think it's better if I hide itI really hope that I survive this

When she done playing, she closes her eyes and draped her head to her folded arms that leaned on the piano, while I look at her, admiring her. Wanting to make my presences known to her, I begin to clap my hands; she jumped a little on the bench a little scared from me clapping. Seeing her jump, does make me regret clapping my hand after.

"Sorry, I didn't mean to scare you. Didn't know you knew how to play?" I tell her with a small smile trying to come off as friendly as possible.

"No, you're good, just didn't know I had an audience looking" she tells me, returning a small smile like the one I gave her.

"You're really good by the way. What song were you sing too?" I ask.

"You probably don't know her but it was by Gracie Abrams," she answers. Yeah, she's right; I don't know who Gracie Abrams is, but I plan on listening to more of her music to see more of what Kyla likes.

"Yeah, haven't heard of her. Sorry-" I go on but am shortly interrupted by her.

"Oh, don't be. It's not everyones cup of tea" she says happily to me. "What's your name? I don't think I ever got it."

"Leo" I answer her as I extend a hand to which she takes.

"Kyla, but you probably knew it," she mumbles back to me looking shyly.

She's not wrong.

"I should let you know that, the food will be ready in an hour if you were going out of here. But your brothers, will have called for you or looked for you. Didn't think you'd like that very much," I say and scratched the back of my head and looked down. I do this when I'm nervous.

"Thanks, was going to leave anyways too" she lets me know as she stands to go to the door of the music room. "Bye" she says as she waves to me and exits the room leaving me alone.

Wow. She seems amazing.

Chapter 16 - Time together

- -

When that boy, Leo, found me in the music room and let me know when dinner was going to be, I was so grateful he had came and told me than one of the boys. Here's the thing: I consciously know they are my brothers; but there's like this barrier between us. They grew up together, I'm an outsider compared to them. I know nothing of them and they know nothing of me. I don't want to get hurt or have high expectations of them, so distancing myself from my dad and them is the best way I can save myself from getting hurt.

They're not my family. They have each other.

I don't need them, and they don't need me.

All I want is my mom right now. She'd tell me what to do and how to best handle this situation. I don't have the simplest idea of what to do with them or how to still process them in my life now. It's not like I really had a choice in being stuck with them. I need that money from my inheritance to pay off my debt with my aunt. My mom would know what is best...

But I'll never have that anymore. She's not here anymore.

Going into my room and being in there for a couple minutes, I come to a realization; and it smacks me in the face, in a metaphorical sense. I might have to spend time with my "brothers" after dinner. Shit. I'll have to figure something out to get out of it; maybe until the foreseeable future, which is... while I'm staying here.

I might get a job to not spend so much time in the house with my dad or the boys. Wait... Where am I going to go to for school? I could tell them that I need to do some after school thing and they'll probably believe me. Right? This is a disaster, but I'll think about it a little more when the time comes. I don't even have a school to go to right now, so there's no safe place yet.

Having set a timer for ten minutes before dinner, I goes off annoyingly. I go to leave my room to go to dinner because I don't want them coming to get me. It's not like I need an escort or something for dinner. Heading down to go to the dining room, I hear voices coming from the living room. I make my way towards the living room, very quietly as to not attract their attention on me and come to see that the boys are lounging on the couch talking to each other.

I feel a pang in my chest seeing them together getting along. All they're doing is talking but it's the way they talk and look at each other that gets to me a little; like a family. My mom, grandma, and I, we'd sometime watch movies while we ate our food and I was so much fun. Most of the time I be commenting about the movie while it was playing - Mom hated it, when I did that but her reaction was so funny. She'd try to get made by making a scowl but it just looked odd on her like a child trying to make a silly face but not quite making it. Looking back at the memory, I laugh to myself a little, and regret it instantly.

My laugh caught the attention of Christian. Seeing him try to figure who laughed and where it came from, leads me to get away from my spot near the living room to the dining room. I get there before everyone and decide to take a seat far from my dad and from the boys as possible; so I end up sitting on the opposite side from my dad's seat but the last seat on the right side of the table where Ryder had an open seat last time at dinner.

As soon as seven o'clock hits, all the boys footsteps are heard coming closer, and closer to the dining room. I sit there trying to act like their entrance doesn't affect me busy looking aimlessly at my phone.

I see that have a couple notifications from my email, but a message catches my eye. From my best friend, Carter. I haven't told him anything that happened; it just happened all too fast. We have told each other everything that happens to us. He's like a brother I didn't have, or at least now a brother I wish I had. I text him back quickly under the table:

Carter

C - Where have you been? I haven't seen you all day

K- so funny story... My dad got out of prison and his mom died so now I have to stay with him for a while... funny am I right?

C - ...

C - K, are you ok?

K - I'm good for now... look I'll call you later gtg (got to go)

While I place my phone on the table, my dad comes into the dining room from his office. He doesn't say anything to me, so I just silently hope he doesn't try to start awkward conversation with me. Not paying attention to anything around me, I don't even notice when the food comes out; there's a lot of food. There's spaghetti, salad, garlic bread, even stuffed bell peppers. Who even cooked all of this food?

"Darlene, does most of the cooking here a long with the cleaning. She works here with her husband, Mauricio, who does all the handiwork and yard work. Then there's their son's, Alexander and Leo, who also live here but Alexander is off at college, so he's not really here that much. Leo, lives he though so you'll probably see him around," whispers Ryder to he almost as reading my thoughts. I nod back at him as a way to indicate that I understood everything he said.

A plate is placed in front of me, to which then I face a woman in her early forties or mid-forties give me a small smile. "I hope you like the food, I made it. Oh, I'm Darlene, by the way" she tells me. I respond to her with a quiet thank you back. I begin to fill my plate with a little of everything, but if I'm being honest with myself I'm not even that hungry. I just don't want them to be fussing over me.

As dinner goes on, everyone is talking amongst each other together. Everyone besides me at least is being seemingly fine. I just want today to be over. Stuffing my face with a piece of garlic bread, Christian so casually drops the agreement we made: to spend time with each other... as siblings.

"Kyla, we're going to watch a movie after dinner. Join us," he says. He's not asking, he's telling me. I remain quiet because I have nothing to say back.

"Yeah, Kie. Our time together that we spend will be so awesome!" Ryder adds a little too loud next to me.

Hearing the nickname Ryder just called me, "Kie", doesn't sit right with me. He doesn't get the privilege to call me that or any nickname as for that matter. The only people that can call me that is Carter, my mom and grandma. Yet, now out of those three people only one remains who can still call me that.

"Don't call me that" I mumble back to him.

"What?" he asks.

"I said don't call me that" I tell him back, having found my voice a bit stronger.

"Why?" he questions.

"It's just a stupid nickname. No big deal," Mason butts; when no one asked or wanted his input.

"Just call me by my name. No nicknames," I retort so that everyone can hear.

This earns me back a small 'got it' from Ryder and a hard glare from Mason. Christian must have seen everything, because turning after feeling a stare coming my way, I find him looking at me. Trying to show that it doesn't affect me, I go back to continue finishing my dinner; so that I can then spend some quality time with my, oh so wonderful, brothers that I know so, so well. Note the sarcasm.

~

~

~

Author's Note: Hey! I'm so sorry everyone for not having updated in a while. I just been so busy with school and work. But I'll try to set a consistent day to update 'Where I Went From Here'.

I hoped you enjoyed this chapter ;)

Chapter 17 - Spending time with Us

After dinner, I had planned to go up to my room to catch up on more work. I was actually going to start on more work that just needed to be done in advance; I had already finished all of what I had to get done for today and most of tomorrow since there wasn't much for me to do and I didn't know what else to do with myself.

I am not by all means obsessed with my job, I'm just use to occupying myself with any work that needs to be done. I work with my dad now at the company that my grandparents had started. The company that they owned was, more or less, a little bit of everything mixed into one; we deal with electronics, clothing, to all sorts of retail stuff. We also have another small company that deals with commerce and international security. Yet, I try to spend my free time with my family. Family is a big part of me; my brothers have been with me for as long as I've been alive, my dad has been present in mine and my brother's life; he would try to make of the best that he could when he went to prison and not lose connection with us; he would try to help us even in prison.

With Kyla, it was different for her. She didn't have siblings by her side through hard times, or her most happiest moments, besides her mother. If I had known about her, I would have made it my goal and job to be there for my sister. I plan on making sure she becomes involved in this family as much as possible. She's now a part of my family, and I'm a part of her family.

While at dinner last night, I overhead some of what was going between Ryder and Kyla. All Ryder did was call Kyla a nickname; Hearing Ryder call Kyla, "Kie", tugged at me a little bit, how he's trying to include her and is trying to warm up to her. Still, she's not even making the effort to try to warm up to us or get to know us at least. Somehow, I knew that this was going to happen with Kyla. That's why I made the rule of her spending time with us; so that we can have a sibling relationship and function as a family.

Tonight I plan, on having Kyla spending time with us for the first time as part of the agreement, I made with her. At the beginning, I know things are going to be awkward especially her; but all I can really do at this point is hope things can go smooth from after this. What are we even going to do with her tonight? We'll just have to figure it out when we're all together.

Shit, I should probably let my brothers know of what's going on later. I'll just message them in our group chat.

~

b. bros

So, tonights plan with Kyla is movie night. I wanted to start with something casual and small for our first time spending quality time together. Movie suggestion will be then too btw. Also NO SKIPPING - C

R - Got it big bro!!!

M - fine

L - Cool beans

E - Sure!

R - Also could we have snack too???

~

Now that it's nighttime, I'm going to head upstairs to get Kyla for our movie night. I had called the boys beforehand so that they could help me setup but I had already gotten everything setup earlier. I just needed in excuse to get their asses downstairs in the movie room and on time. I even asked Leo, if he wanted to join us to which he eagerly accepted; don't know why though.

Standing at in front of Kyla's door, I grow anxious. The certainty of tonight is what is gnawing me. Still, a part of me that's a tiny bit excited is what allows me to knock on her door. I'm about to knock in her door again but suddenly he hear the doorknob turning and then I see Kyla.

This is going to be such a great night.

~

~

~

A/N: Hello everyone! I just wanted to say I'm so sorry for not posting it updating. School is just getting to me but hopefully I'll have another update this week or by Monday.Would you like to see a love interest involved or some drama?? Let me know... till next time.

Hope you enjoyed :)

Chapter 18 - Movie Night

POV - Kyla Bower ~

Just as I'm about to begin to wind down for the night, I get a knock on my door and it hits me that tonight's the night is when my wonderful siblings and I will have "sibling bonding" time. Note the sarcasm. However, when I open my door the person there is the last person I expect to be knocking on my door. Christian. With the door ajar, we stand there silently looking at each other; neither of us going to say anything. Seeing that neither of us plan to start talking, I go to say something at the same time Christian opens his mouth. I quickly shut my mouth but he motions for me to speak first.

"Err... How can I help you?" I ask him as I shift from foot to the other. As if sensing my discomfort, Christian suddenly says, "You don't have to nervous. I just came to get you so that the boys, you, and me could spend some time together with a movie night". In a calm voice he adds as he takes a few spends away from the door, "You coming? Remember you agreed" as he waves to me to follow him.

I realize then and there that with Christian's term of spending time with my half-brothers, is that he will hold it over my head that I agreed to it; and I'll have to hold my end of our deal to the end.

"Yes I remember. Shall we then," I say with a raised brow.

Here goes nothing...

Once downstairs in the movie room with Christian, I come to find that all my other half-brothers are there; plus Leo, too. How nice. Going to sit down, I try to sit the farthest away from them but to my dismay, Ryder chooses to sit next to me on one side and to my other, Leo. Ryder seems to be making himself comfortable by gathering blankets, a bunch of candy, and a big bowl of popcorn. Still stuck on staring at Ryder, I feel something being placed on my lap; and come to see that Leo had gotten a blanket to share and small bowls of popcorn each of us. Grateful that he was considerate of me, I return a thank you to him with a small smile to which he acknowledged me in with a small nod.

"So, Kyla since this is your first movie night with us, you get to pick the movie," Ryder announce happily to me but narrows his eyes to Leo slightly. I don't even want to watch a movie right now which is why I respond back to him as, "I don't really care what movie we watch. You can pick the movie, just nothing scary".

His smile falls just a little but then regains his smile from before. "Fine, then. But don't complain if ya'll don't like the movie I pick."

After a long indecisive decision making, Ryder picks some Marvel movie with robots trying to get back at Ironman or whatnot. Then, I feel an elbow nudge coming from my side where Leo is sitting; I turn to him and mouth a 'what?' to him to which he nudges me again but this time with a box of candy as if to pay attention to the movie. I just shake my head and roll my eyes. This is what he wanted to tell me.

"I mean have some candy," Leo whispers in my ear. Oh, this what he meant.

I shake my head and reluctantly return my attention to the movie which I was then gaining interest. Nudge again. Growing a little irritated, I face him again full on to see what he wants this time.

"I don't want anything" I begrudgingly say back to him.

"Come on, you know you want some candy," he tells me as he playfully waves a carton of candy in my face; at this I begin to giggle. Still giggling, I roll my eyes to him trying to match the same playfulness he had.

"Fine, but pass me the watermelon Sour Patches." As he passes me the box of gummies, I pinch his side. That's what he gets for being annoying. "Ow! Hey what was that for?"

"That was for not giving me, my candy sooner." He proceeds to pinch me back as payback. This then brakes a fit of pinching and laughter from both, Leo and I. My stomach is hurting so much from all the laughing that I've done that I have to stop and so does Leo. We don't even notice that the movie had ended and the credits are rolling. With our laughter coming to an end, I feel eyes on Leo and me. Slowing turning my head, I see that Ryder, Levi, and Elijah are staring at us. But as soon, as I turned to look at the boys Christian and Mason quickly turned their heads so that I wouldn't catch them looking. Well, this is getting awkward.

"Um, so this was fun!" I say to break the awkwardness in the air, but a little too enthusiastically. "So, I think I am going to head up to bed. Night" I add as I stand, pointing with my thumbs to the door behind my back.

"Me too" announces Leo. "Good night guys" he adds with a wave.

~

Quietly walking down the hallway, Leo turns to face me and tells me, "I had a fun time, hope you did you too."

"Yeah, I did. Thank to you mostly" I tell him with a smile. Once in my room and in bed, I stare up at the ceiling go over how the night went.

"What an eventful night," I say in a whisper to myself.

~

~

~

A/N - Hello all! I am so deeply sorry for noting having posted an update in a while, but with finals coming up at school and work it's been a little too much. But spring break it coming up so... yeah.

I hope you liked this chapter :)

Chapter 19 - Mothers' Dinner Party

One week later

A whole week has passed since the last Friday, my half-brothers and I spent some "sibling bonding". Christian had told me yesterday that we had o cancel our time together because everyone was busy; from dad, Christian, Elijah with work at the company. To Levi with a special commission painting, Mason with classes and football, along with Ryder with something super busy he had to do with some friends. Therefore, I was left all to myself. Yippie me.

Now dinner has started, so as I hurry downstairs to get my seat that I've self assigned myself, I see Mason cutting me off by going in front of me while Levi just walk by my side. I don't understand why the fuck he hates me so much, when I haven't done anything to him. Once situated on the dining table with almost everyone present, we just wait for Christian so that dinner can start.

Idly seated, I wonder into my own thoughts on how much has gone since my mom and grandma died; I went from barely able to carry on with myself to having seeing my dad for the first time in twelve years to inheriting so much. Plus, no one in this house knows that mom died, I've made dad at least believe that she know's I'm here with them and that completely fine with me spending time with all of them. There was this one time, dad wanted to call mom to let her know and to talk to her about some important stuff, but I immediately told him that I'd do it; that it was most likely that she'd like to hear it from me than him, who hadn't seen or talked to her in years. So after there has been no questioning about my mother by the boys or dad.

It's just been crazy. Hearing footsteps coming closer and closer to the dining room, is what brings me out of my thoughts. Not even a second passes as Christian barely sits, when the rest of the boys go at it with the food. I make no move to get caught up in the entanglement of arms trying to grab of pass dishes; I just go for the closest plate of food to me which is the Caesar salad, when every had their plates filled with some combination of food, I then go for the lasagna and snatch a piece of bread quickly on my plate. Elijah sees me do this and makes a "did you seriously just do that" face; seeming him do that makes me giggle a little too loudly and catches everyone's attention.

"You good, Kyla?" Ryder asks amusingly.

Clearing my throat, I answer him "no".

Dinner goes by smoothly, with dad and the boys making conversation amongst each other while I try to stay out of it; but they still try to include me. Ryder tries the most to make conversation with me and I actually... don't mind it whatsoever. It's kind of nice. I don't say much, but Ryder, man, says plenty for the both of us; he talks about a little of everything.

Like movies, shows, places, and music. Especially music, he loves music and formed a band with his most close friends.

Still listening to Ryder ramble on about how one of his friends was a dumbass almost breaking his foot on his skateboard, gets interrupted mid sentence by someone not so subtly clearing their throat. We both turn at the same time to see so see that the culprit was Elijah who then turns to Christian.

"Kyla, we wanted to ask if you could join all of us to go to our mothers' dinner party?" Christian asks.

"Why?" I defensively respond.

"They'd like to meet you. Since you're our sister they just want to get to know you a little, and see you in person" he continues to go on.

"They? As in both of your guys mothers" I inquire.

"Yes" Christian says with confused face.

"Oh. Um.. I don't know" I says hesitantly.

Christian lets it go but I see that glint of sadness in his eyes. Turing to continue my dinner, I turn in time to see Ryder and see that he has a little disappointment in his eyes. Seeing this I feel bad, their mothers seem scary and I don't want to have to deal with them in anyway shape of form.

With dinner done, I head to my room feeling mentally exhausted for no particular reason. In the comfort of my room, I begin to get ready for bed; even if I end up not get much sleep, I just want to be in bed. Showered and in my pajamas, I go to lay down but as I'm fixing my blankets on myself I get a knock on my door. Reluctantly I give a tired 'come in' so that whoever it is knocking can come in and let me sleep.

Not so surprised it turns out to be Ryder the one who knocked. He rapidly enter my room and makes a beeline to the my bed and plops down to my side. Making himself comfortable on my bed, I have to readjust myself and sit as I tun to face him feeling slightly annoyed.

"Ryder, what do you want?" I whine to him.

"Do you really not want to have dinner with our mothers'? Not even meet them? Aren't you curious about them?" he bombards me with question after question.

"I not that curious about them, I could get to know them vicariously from others and meet them far away at some point or something. But I just don't know, okay. I don't know" I spill out my mini rant.

He turns to face me becoming serious in his expression. "Look, I get it. They're new people who so happen to be the mothers' of your brothers, but they're not bad people. Yes, they can both be a lot to handle and say stuff without filter but they're just fine I guess as mom's go... Plus, I'd really like for you to meet them. You're my sister and even though we've just meet a month or a couple of weeks ago, you mean a lot to me. So please think about it?"

"Okay, I'll think about it" I mumble as I respond.

"Thanks, lil' sis" he says as he goes back to his happy, bright self.

"If it makes you feel a little better, I'd also like to meet your mom one day" he states already off my bed with his hand to the door; and with that said he leaves.

Hearing him say that he'd like to meet my mom, makes my heart ache. It would've been nice to see Ryder and my mom. It's sad think think of the what-if's or the would've been's, but Ryder is starting to grow on me... so

I'll at least try for his sake. Only his sake. With Ryder's words in mind, I slowly feel my eyes growing heavier and heavier growing me into sleep.

~

In the morning, I anxiously wait for Ryder to come down. I just sit in the living room with the TV on, not really paying any attention to what's on the screen. At breakfast, Ryder is the last to come down to my dismay. When he's comfortable enough in his chair, eating breakfast I pat him on the shoulder to gain his attention. Ryder turn to look at me, and I motion for him to come a little closer to me so that I can tell him something. He brings his ear close to my face but before that I take a deep breathe.

"I'll do it" I whisper only his ears.

"You'll do what?" he asks confused.

"I'll go with all of you to have dinner with your mothers'" I whisper again but somehow managing to whisper even lowly. This earns me a check ear to ear grin from him.

"Thank you, thank you, thank you, lil' sis."

Oh, what have I gotten myself into...

~

~

~

A/N: Hello, everyone!!! I hope you all have had a good week! Unlike mine where I was busy with finals so yeah... But moving on, what do you think will happen next? What do think the mothers' will be like? Till next time.

Hope you enjoyed this chapter :)

Chapter 20 - Lorna & Brianne

- -

~ POV: Kyla Bower ~

A few days had passed since the dinner party was mentioned, and nothing had been said to me afterwords. Apparently, the mothers', Lorna and Brianne, wanted everything to go "accordingly", whatever that meant. I had asked Ryder what that meant and all he said was that I'd see soon, but the only thing he failed to tell me was that soon, was going to be tonight. So now my predicaments are the mothers' and what to wear tonight.

I honestly could give two fucks on what to wear for them, but I don't want to let Ryder down; I promised him, and I can't back out of it now. He seemed so happy when I told me I'd do it, and when he hugged me it had been the first time in awhile that I had felt comfortable with someone. Whenever I'm with Ryder, he makes me feel not so lonely... and there are times where I just want to spill the whole truth of my life to him; from growing up, to my mom and grandma, the accident, being by myself, to working multiple jobs, and so on. Yet, I can't tell him or rather anyone for that matter. Too many questions will be asked and I don't think I can answer them for them.

~

~ POV: Third Person ~

Inside her room, Kyla was in her closet with heaps of clothes on the floor trying to find something decent-looking to wear tonight. She had spent so much time procrastinating looking for an outfit, that she had just spent her time in bed watching a movie, going on a FaceTime with Carter, and scrolling through Instagram. Now standing, Kyla just stood staring at her closet and at the ground. A knock at her room, is what brought her out of staring contest with her closet; Flustered, she scurried to to door to see who it was on the other side of the door.

"Coming" she yelled as she was running to door but tripped over herself. On the other side of the door stood Elijah, a little amused after hearing the a yelp from his little sister on the other side; He had went up to her room to tell her that the dinner party was going in a couple hours but that they were leaving at 6:30pm. Opening the door, Kyla tried to appear that nothing had happened but upon seeing Elijah's failed attempted on covering his laugh, she knew that he had heard her fall.

"Yep. What can I do for you?" She said to him as if nothing.

"Someone's a little flustered, I see" he commented amusingly.

"Hmm, didn't notice. So?" she retorted sarcastically. Deciding to mess with Kyla, he continued with her sarcasm.

"I guess I won't tell you anything, anymore" he said as he pretended to walk away.

"What is it?"

"Hm... oh nothing"

"Come on! Tell me!" she whined to him.

"OK then, I'll tell you. We're going to leave at 6:30 to go to our mothers' house" and with that said from Elijah he turned to go back downstairs with his dad and brothers.

I only have a couple hours to get ready. Shit, Kyla thought to herself.

~

~ POV: Kyla Bower ~

Already dressed, in a simply dress I found with a cardigan and some heels, I stare at myself in the full length mirror in my room; not recognizing myself for a second. I haven't gotten dressed up since my mom and grandma's funeral. I even put on some makeup to look presentable. Tonight could result in two ways: lively and joyful or up in ruins. I just hope that it doesn't go bad or anything.

"Kyla, come on" I hear coming from downstairs.

"Going" I yell. I quickly grab my black crossbody purse and phone and booked it downstairs. I didn't even see what was in front of me, since my focus was on my feet and the stairs steps so that I wouldn't fall; till I hit a someone's back, face first. From the impact, I stumbled back a little but luckily someone grabbed my wrist to steady me. Looking up, I see that Mason had been the one that I came in contact with... and he looked at me annoyed. "Thanks" I mumbled to him, to which he responded back to me with a grunt.

We were then all divided into 2 different cars. Now with dad, Levi, Christian, and Mason; and the other with Elijah, Ryder, and me. It was originally going to be Elijah, Mason, and me, but Ryder easily convinced Mason to switch with him. I did't take much convincing Mason; he doesn't want to be anywhere near me and he's made it very obvious. I just try to ignore him. Before we had gotten situated into the cars, Ryder had whispered in my ear that he come in the car I'd be going in "to prep me for their mothers'". Their mothers' must be a lot to handle, I thought to myself.

Now at the front of a beautiful two-story house, we all stood there waiting to be let inside. During our drive here, Ryder had told me so much to know about their mothers. More than I even wanted to know, if I'm being honest. He told me that Brianne, Mason and his mom, doesn't like being people chewing loudly, or when phones are on the table; and Lorna, Christian, Elijah and Levi's mom, dislikes it when their are side conversations at the dinner table and can say stuff without much thought.

So, with that information in mind, I knew that I ultimately had to watch myself from them.

~

(Time skip to being at the dinner table)

When Lorna and Brianne, had opened the door for us they immediately when to each their sons'. They embraced them with hugs and kisses that it was uncomfortable to see. I was basically pushed to the side and watched their interaction. Guess dad must have seen how I was looking with them that he tried to give me a side hug, but I just turned away to go and greet them. Seeing my half-brothers and their mothers', made me miss mom even more.

"You must be Kyla" pointed out Lorna. I shyly nodded my head to her observation. "Hm.. You're different to what I imagined" commented Brianne.

"It's a pleasure to meet you" I told them while extending my hand to shake theirs. I didn't know what else to do, this was all so nerve-wracking.

With all the greeting aside, we were all hurriedly moved to the dinner table where all the food was placed neatly on the table. All the boys and dad went to their seats, like they'd done this so many times; which them might have, and I was left standing by myself once more.

"Kyla, come sit next to me" exclaimed Ryder a little too loud. I complied and seat next to him with Mason to my other side and Christian in front of me. Goody me to be sitting close to those two.

"So, shall we get started then" announced Lorna and Brianne closely at the same time, looking directly my way.

Yep, this is going to bad.

~

^Kyla's outfit

~

~

~

A/N: The mother's have something planned up their sleeves... till next time!

Hope you enjoyed this chapter ;)

Chapter 21 - Dinner Party

"So, shall we get started then" announced Lorna and Brianne closely at the same time, looking directly my way.

~ POV: Kyla Bower ~

Everyone but me got their plates ready and piled them with food. The food that Lorna and Brianne 'requested' from their cook was mostly a variety of pastas, some salads, and dishes that the boys like; That was their words when they were explaining the food for tonight. As the boys, dad, and the mom's begin to eat, I can't help but stare at them at how all this seems normal to them. Maybe in an alternate reality my mom and me, and maybe my grandma would be get a long with all of them. I wouldn't have had to grow up not knowing my half-brothers, or - Click!

Getting out of my thoughts, I look to see you made the noise. Not seeing who made the clicking noise, I go back to finally getting food on my plate. Throat clear. Ugh. Who the fuck is doing that! Someone kicks my foot from my right, I turn to Ryder with a 'what do want?' face and he gestures to Lorna. Trying to appear like unfazed, I focus on Lorna, who's giving me a forced smile that doesn't suit her at all.

"Um. Yes?" I ask not knowing what to say.

"As I was saying, if I had known what foods you liked, Kyla, I would have asked for it to be made. But even then, with the amount of food on the table it's fine with what we have" she proceeds in an annoyingly fake sweet tone.

"Oh, it's completely fine. Like you said, with all this food we're fine" I say with a fake smile to reciprocate her's. Even if she knew what I liked to eat, she wouldn't have done anything with knowing about it. She spelled it out clearly: you don't matter to me.

"Well, we hope all of you enjoy it. We wanted it to be special!" Brianne announces.

I don't have that much of an appetite. Being here with the boys mothers's sucked the life and energy out of me, but in order to not gain their attention I nibble on some salad. While I eat, Christian, Levi, and dad form some light conversation between Lorna and Brianne; therefore, leaving me the perfect opportunity to tune everyone and everything. Almost everyone but Ryder.

Ryder grabs a plate of what seems like cubed beef in some sort of roast, claiming that I should try it. With my fork, I stab into a piece and put it into my mouth. He must see the shock on my face because it's surprisingly delicious. I eat meats, but sometimes I don't like the way it looks or the way it tastes; so there are time's that it can be hard to eat it, but this is amazing.

"It's my favorite! I knew that you'd like it at least" he says mostly to himself pridefully but a little too loud to the point where it gain everyone's atten tion... and unfortunately makes Lorna and Brianne's interest peak.

"That's good dear! Now, Kyla why don't you tell us a little bit about your- self to us. Besides we're family now, and family should know everything but that's won't be happening in your case at least," she states putting heavy emphasize on 'family'.

Hearing her say this makes me feel even more uncomfortable than I already was, making me squirm in my seat. Levi makes a motion for me with his head to go on. Taking in a deep breath, I give a brief introduction of myself, " Well, my name's Kyla." snicker. I keep on going; "I'm 16, a sophomore in high school."

"Oh my! I can tell that you're a girl of few words" comments Brianne. Lorna, sneers as she adds "Her mother must have done all the talking for her." At the mention of my mother, I shoot my gaze with drawn brows at Lorna and Brianne, looking between them. "What did you say about my mother?" I ask not sure if I heard correctly.

"Your mother. She must have done all the talking for you. I mean with her sweet mouth she must have gotten all the attention from others," Lorna carries on but most define referring to others as men; while, Brianne doesn't stop. "That's how she got Richard's back then. What about now, Kyla? how many people chase after - "

"Lorna!" my dad cuts her off.

"Don't you talk about my mother like that" I say coldly. More cold than I intended to, but I don't care. The audacity that these grown ass women have to hold a grudge against my mom of something that must have happened years ago. I see that they're doing. They're trying to belittle me for something my mom did that I had not control over.

Silence.

Silence envelopes the whole dining room.

"Ha! A feisty little thing, you are" Brianne notes breaking the silence.

"Oh, Kyla! Lighten up! I'm just saying the truth. Anyhow, it's not like your mother's dead" Lorna voices.

With that last sentence coming from her mouth, is what breaks the last straw I've been having to endure these bitches during this whole dinner. This dinner party that they invited me too, might I add. I put up with all there mockery, and teasing about my mom and me; but Lorna just crossed a line she didn't even know existed when she talked about my mother and death in one sentence.

And with that I'm done.

With both of them, maybe even all of them.

Abruptly, I stand out of my seat making the chair scrape the polished hard wood floors. Everyone's eyes are on me at this point. I turn my whole body to face both, Lorna and Brianne, who've been acting like a pair of jealous girls my age would act instead of their own age.

"I've sat throughout this whole dinner listening to the crap that has come out of both of your mouths. And I'm done with your shit!" I say as my voices raised. I tried to say it in a calmly manner, but my emotions just got the best of me.

"Kyl-" Levi starts to say but I don't give him the chance to even finish what he was going to say. At some point, Ryder also stood up and put him hand on my shoulder but I just shrugged it off. Sorry, Ryder but I don't have time for you right now.

"No! No. They don't know anything what they're saying...and neither do you guys" I spout back.

"I'd say that all this, the dinner was lovely. But I can say that since it's be a lie. Thank you anyways," I finish. Yet, I had to bite my tongue to not say that meeting them was fuckin' awful. I said what I had to say, so I push myself from the table and run to front door.

Before leaving, I stop to the coat room, where they had us all take off our sweaters and jackets, and sneak my hand to Christian's jacket. With his car keys successfully in my hand, I go out the door and slam it shut. Still, hearing a little of what was said before.

"Kyla! Come back!" my dad shouted for me.

"Oh, Richard! Just leave her go, clearly her mother didn't raise her right" Lorna says.

"Such an ungrateful child" Brianne adds.

~

Once I'm in Christian's car, I speed my way through the streets until I get to the mansion. With tears running down my check, and occasionally blurring my vision, I don't even realize I had arrived at the mansion. Running up the steps and throwing the door open, I don't even bother closing it as I try to go to my room.

Opening my room, I step in, shut and lock my door; then lunge myself to my bed and bury my face in my pillow, and grab a picture I have of my mother, grandma, and me from my nightstand; holding it closely to me as I cry for everything. For the way I was treat at dinner, for being alone, for having to work making things workout for myself, but mostly for my mom and grandma not being with me.

~

I hadn't even heard when the boys and dad came back. The only indication that they had came back was Ryder knocking on my door.

"Kyla, please. Can we talk?" He asked at my door. I wanted to be by myself with my emotions and my mom, even if it was just her picture; so I didn't answer him.

"Please, Kyla."

When he realized, I wasn't going to answer or open the door for him, was when he gave up.

"I get it. It's been a long night, so good night then. See you in the morning."

I wish the morning wouldn't come.

Chapter 22 - Lingering in Thought

~ POV: Third Person~

After Kyla had left, shortly after the boys and Richard left from Lorna and Brianne's house too. They were all silent in the car rides back to the estate, all lingering in thought to what Kyla had said earlier.

"They don't know anything what they're saying...and neither do you guys"

That's what she had said... and there was no faking it, not even if they wanted to because it was the truth; and the truth can't be denied.

Once at the estate, they all get out of the cars and start to make their way to the door, that was still unlocked from when Kyla had came back. Without a single words from either of them, they headed on their own ways. The boys to each of their rooms, and Richard to his office, each of them stuck in their own thoughts but had one thing, or rather someone who was the main focus of their thought. That someone being Kyla.

The youngest of the brothers, Ryder, was thinking about how much he pushed, and pushed, Kyla to go meet his brothers' mother, Lorna, and his mother without thinking of the repercussions of what could happen; when in reality he wasn't think about Kyla, but more about what he wanted. He knew he made to make it up to her, somehow.

Mason, was thinking about Kyla's breakdown. Each word was replaying in his head of what was said in the interaction between Kyla, Lorna, and his mother. I should have stepped in when it was getting heated, he thought. Still, he didn't know why he couldn't or hadn't in that moment. He heard and saw how much effort his brothers were trying with Kyla, but for him it was like their was a stone wall that was built between them; and he knew that it was placed there by him. He wanted to truly apologize to her, because in his own way he care for her; he wasn't;t good for her in anyway. Even if he was distant with her, because he was trying to save her from himself.

Levi, had no words in him. He hadn't a single clue of what had gone on at dinner, or at what point things had gone sideways. He cared for Kyla. Although, he wasn't as close to Kyla as he wanted or like to be, he was going to work on that. Typically, he was a laidback brother, but with Kyla he needed to be present for her; and he would try.

Unlike, his brothers who were think about dinner. Elijah was working on a plan or rather a way for Kyla and him to, somehow start off on a clean slate. Elijah wasn't oblivious about Kyla; he noticed the way she needed them at dinner to set in, but like dumbasses didn't. Elijah knew that Kyla deserved more from him, his brothers, and father. If his brothers or dad were going to set up for Kyla, he would. He would do it for her.

The eldest brother, Christian, was disappointed. Not at Kyla, but at himself, and his father. But he was mainly enraged with his mother, for treating Kyla, that way she treated her at dinner. Kyla had not done anything to her in anyway, yet his mother blamed her for things that happened in the past. Kyla, is just a girl that is dealing with a chaotic situation that she shouldn't be dealing with for her age, or anywho should be dealing with. Even if he didn't show it, Christian was proud of Kyla. She didn't put up with the shit his mother or Brianne through her way, she didn't back down.

In his office, Richard, was angry at himself (as he should), for not being there for his daughter. She needed him and he hadn't shown up to have her back. He was speechless at dinner. He was a shitty father. Quietly, walking out of his office, his feet had dragged him in front of Kyla's bedroom door. There was no sound coming from her room, yet he just rested his forehead on the door. Kyla deserved better than him he thought.

Things between the boys and Richard needed to change. Not for them but for Kyla.

Chapter 23 - Aftermath

~ POV: Kyla Bower ~

Morning came too soon.

I couldn't get a wink of sleep last night. My mind would not allow me to go to sleep; it kept replaying, Lorna and Brianne's words about my mother and me. They were so cruel for no valid reason that I could think of, besides being jealous women. The sad thing is that they judged me without even knowing what I've been through.

I heard what Ryder said to me through my closed door. I appreciate what he said, but it doesn't change the fact that it all happened on his mother and Lorna's end. I don't blame him or resent him for something that he didn't do.

"it's not like your mother's dead"

Shake my head and mind from those thoughts, I decide to get out of bed and open my door just a smidge to listen if anyone is downstairs. Not hearing anything, I just assume that everyone is still asleep after yesterday. I quickly get ready and pack my backpack. Trying to get Lorna's words out of my head, I decided that I'd go out myself; to have a day to myself without anyone of the male species that live in this house with me, who you might be thinking? Well, it's my half-brothers and dad.

I step out of my room, with my keys in my hand so gracefully attempting not to make noise. On my way downstairs to the garage, I thought I had did it; I had manage to not bump into any of the boys... however, I was sorely mistaken. Grabbing a pair of car keys from the garage, Leo seemed to magically appear before me.

Without wasting any second more, I pressed the car key's alarm to find the car and made a beeline to the car. As I got situated in the car, I rolled the window down to a now confused Leo, making a 'shush' gestures with my pointer finger to my mouth.

"You didn't see me. You didn't hear anything. Got it? Cool" were the last words I said to him as I made my way out of the garage to the main streets.

~

Not having planned out my day, I had stumbled on a small road with some stores. In a coffee shop, I had gotten a message from Leo, letting me know that he didn't say anything but that the boys were asking for me. I ventured into a couple of the stores, and ended up buying 2 books a a cute bookstore.

The sad part of this day is going back to the estate to reality.

~

A moment hadn't passed when I stepped into the house, when Ryder embraced me into a hug. his hug made me smile, and unconsciously I hugged him back.

"I know you went out" he whispered into my ear. I playfully stoved him away, silently laughing.

"And what about it?" I say sarcastically.

"Nothing... but you should come to the living room after you drop off your things in your room. The rest think you just locked yourself in your room," he informed me.

~

"So how was your day, Kyla?" questioned Elijah as I sat down on the couch after taking my things to my room.

If Ryder's interpretation of 'they think you've been in your room all along' is an underlying implication that they all know I was out is this... then I'm probably fucked. They're not getting anything out of me though.

"It's been fine, calm. Been reading mostly," I answer him nonchalantly. As I'm finished talking dad, comes into the living room looking a little tired. He doesn't sit on the couch until he spots me, his shoulders visibly relax a little.

"So... what's this all about?" I ask.

"I wanted to talk about last night, the dinner party, about what you said," dad replies.

"Look, personally I think last night was a disaster. But I think the best would be to avoid being in the same room with Lorna and Brianne, no offense to you guys. I'm mainly saying this because I'm doing it for myself. I'm sorry I took off, I just need to leave, I know when and where I'm unwanted" I mumble the last part and continue. "And I said a lot last night, so you'll have to be a little more specific to me."

After my little mini-rant, none of the boys say anything but when I turn to look at Levi who's sitting to one side of me; he gives me a small smile and shake his head. He then, mouths 'it's not okay'. I look about him, slightly confused.

What don't they get? I'm pretty sure I was clear and assertive.

"Kyla, what happened was not fine in any way. Like you said it was a disasters. It's safe to say it was a complete shit show. But please. Please, don't downplay how it made you feel," dad says in a softer tone.

"I'm no-" I begin to say but dad cuts me off.

"Let me finish please. Lorna and Brianne were out of place. They shouldn't have said any of those things that they did to you or about you mom. I'm sorry. I'm sorry I didn't say anything or had your back. There's no excuse. You had every right to leave. And I'm glad you did leave. I'm proud you did, actually."

I'm shocked by dad's words. I never would've expected him to say this.

"You stood your ground. You did that by yourself. But Kyla, some of the things that Lorna brought up did make me question somethings... especially when they bought up your mother. I know I agreed to what you asked of me to not get in contact with her, your our child. There's things we need to work out if your going to be staying here.... Does she know your staying here? With me? With us? Has she given you permission to be here? Because Kyla, if she doesn't... she has to know. I have to tell her or you have to tell her."

"No" I say dead flat.

"What do you means no?" asks Levi.

"No, to what? That she doesn't know your staying here? Or no to she had given you permission? Or n-" dad rambles question after question to me.

"No!" I say as I raise my voice.

I can feel my hear beating quickly in my chest. I'm shaking a little, and it's getting a little hard to breathe.

"Kyla, give us something to work with" Ryder pleads.

"No, no, no" I repeat over and over again while my right hand cliches my chest.

"We don't understand what you mean, Ky-" Christian starts to say.

"Don't you get it you can't! You can't talk to my mom! She won't ever answer you, you won't ever see her because- because... SHE'S DEAD!" I shout as a continue to sob. I couldn't hold it me any longer.

I'm sorry mom.

~

~

~

A/N: Hello everyone! I'm so sorry I haven't posted I've been so busy with midterms and final coming up that it's been a mess. I hope this makes up for it though.

What your favorite read currently? Let me know!

I hope you enjoyed reading this chapter :)

Chapter 23 - Aftermath: Part II

"We don't understand what you mean, Ky-" Christian starts to say.

"Don't you get it you can't! You can't talk to my mom! She won't ever answer you, you won't ever see her because- because... SHE'S DEAD!"

~ POV: Richard Bower ~

It couldn't be. It can't be. I think I heard wrong.

Yet, the deafening silence doesn't help contrast what Kyla said.

"What? What did you say?" I question still not quite being able to wrap this newfound information around my head.

Kyla wraps her arms around her middle, almost as an attempt to shield herself; Ryder, being a little more close with her, tries to come near her to give her a hug, however when she notices him coming close to her, she steps back a little. A whimper comes out of her.

"S-She's de-d-dead" she stutters in a small voice.

I can't believe it.

Mary.

Not Mary...

Mary, she can't...

Mary can't be dead.

From my standing position, I falter and grab a hold of the nearest object next to me; so that my knees don't give out. I feel like something is stuck in my throat, not allowing any air to enter my lungs. This is too much. How didn't I know? Why wasn't I made aware? Mary and me had so made plans and things we wanted to do together.

Those will never happen.

I will never see her again.

At this moment, I don't want to think too much about the fact that she's dead, I can't quite think about it too, much because I feel like at any moment I'll breakdown. If I breakdown, I don't know how I'll be able to get back to how I was before knowing Mary is dead. Knowing this, won't change the inevitable, that it's true. What hurt's is that I couldn't be there for her or Kyla, if she needed me because I was stuff in a cell. But what about Kyla? She must have carried this with her for how ever much time has passed since Mary's death. I need to be strong, but not for me; for Kyla.

Kyla needs me.

"But... how?" Levi says, but it seems more to himself.

"How'd your mom die, Kyla?" asks Christian making his tone come out as soft, and calm. The softest, I've ever heard from him ever. Kyla shakes her head with her gaze elsewhere. She doesn't want to talk about it.

"Christian, stop" I start to say but he cuts me off mid sentence.

"How, Kyla?" he asks again.

"Christian!" I shout.

"I- We were going somewhere kind of far from where we use to live in the car. When it was time to turn, I-I g-guess, she couldn't so we continued to go straight. She, she mustn't wanted to freak my grandma or me out so she stayed calm; but as we still went straight and a mountain was getting close and close, she couldn't stay quiet. My grandma and my mom were talking too low for me to hear anything, but when they did, they told me to up out of the car they said so." Kyla tells.

"I didn't want to. I told them, no, that I wouldn't but they made me do it. My mom said that everything would be okay. They said they'd be right behind me. But they lied! They weren't;t behind me!" She finishes as she starts to cry, sobbing.

My baby. I feel so stupid, and worthless, that I knew nothing. I go to Kyla, hug her and bring her closer to me. I could have lost her too, as I lost Mary.

"Do you know why the car couldn't turn?" questions Elijah to her. In my arms, I feel Kyla shake her head.

"I-I- I didn't know. I didn-n't kn-" She says but chokes on the end. I move Kyla a little so I can get a better look at her face. She holds her chest and shirt with her right hand, with her other hand gripping my forearm, struggling to breathe.

She's having a panic attack.

"What's wrong?" inquires Ryder.

"She's having a panic attack" informs Mason in a hoarse voice.

"Try to breathe for me, baby" I beg her. She shakes her head, no. Mason makes his way to my side, and gains Kyla's attention as she moves her eyes to him.

"Tell me five things you see" he ask her.

"D-Dad-d, you-u, Ry-yder" but she can't seem to get more words out as she begins to hyperventilate.

"I-I-I c-ca-can't" She says between breaths. The grip she had on my forearms starts to slip. Without, warning she comes forward with closed eyes. I manage to catch her be in my arms and reposition her with her head on the nook of my shoulder and neck. I hold her so close and tight to me, scared that she'll leave or disappear from me.

Holding her for a while, I stand with her in my arms in a bridal style hold as I take her to her room. Once, I've laid her on her bed and covered her with her blanket, I move some hair from her face and just hold her hand. I place a kiss to her forehead.

"I'm so, so sorry. for not being there for you. For being a shitty dad" I whisper to her.

I'm a shitty dad.

I don't deserve you.

~

~

~

A/N: Hello, everyone! How's everyone's week been so far? Any finals ? Anyway, summer here!!! (or coming close for some of others!!!) Either way, here's a new update...

Hope you enjoyed reading :)

Chapter 24 - Somber Birthday

Waking up with a pounding headache, I open my eyes but immediately shut them tight. The sunlight coming through the windows too bright; I begin to stretch my limbs and ever so slowly open my eyes again, just this time I am successfully able to completely open them. Shifting in my bed, I bury my face in my pillow as last nights events run through my mind; finally telling the truth of my mom and grandma, having a breakdown, and a panic attack in front of my half brothers and dad. Last night was a fucking shit show. Finally, to top of what a mindfuck last night was, today's my birthday.

My first birthday without my mom and grandma.

Although, I've been saying I'm 16 to almost everyone, technically today I'm officially sixteen; I just considered myself a month or two before my birthday. Still lying in bed, I know I have to get up.

Without bothering to get ready immediately, I put on my slippers and head down; to the kitchen starving like a marvin. Downstairs, there is no one, it's dead silent. Fine for me.

Seeing as there's no one to bother me, I decide to make myself some breakfast. When I was younger, my mom started this somewhat tradition for birthdays where the birthday person got a big birthday breakfast. Reminiscing on those times, I go to pantry to grab some pancake mix. Halfway through making my breakfast feast, Mason came down first with Ryder trailing right behind him a couple steps away. I wouldn't have noticed Mason coming towards the kitchen, if it weren't for Ryder's voice talking about how good the house smelt.

"So....whatcha making?" Ryder asked drawing out for no reason. Frankly, I wasn't in the mood to explain why I was making pancakes, or for what.

"I'm just making some breakfast," I replied was a shrug. From my peripheral vision, I saw how Mason was just staring at me; it mostly look like he was analyzing me, as if he knew there was a deeper meaning to what this breakfast I was making held. Truth be told, I wanted a hole to swallow me than have to face Mason. He hasn't been all that nice to me since the moment I stepped foot into this house. Yet, the first time of me being vulnerable and on top of that having a panic attack, he starts to care? Makes no sense to me.

"What's going on here?" Levi asks coming to the kitchen bar where Ryder send Mason are seated. Just as I'm about to answer Christian, Elijah and dad all come too.

"So where's the party going to be?" Dad tosses out casually. Then turns to come to me and gives me a small smile asking me how my night was and if I'm okay, to which I inform him that I'm fine.

"Happy birthday, Kyla. Don't ever don't that I've forgotten about you or the day you were born" he tells me the last part in a low voice for only me to hear. I lower my head at shyness and feel my cheeks getting hotter so that no one can see, still earning an 'aw' from Ryder. When my shyness has passed, all the boys look at me with happiness and shock. However, all of the boys, dumbfounded, with this new information stare at me making me squirm under their eyes.

"What?!" shouts Ryder.

"Oh, you'll be in for a treat" whispers Elijah as he passes by me to get a mug for coffee, and quickly plucks a kiss on the side of my temple. I steal a glance at both Christian and Levi, who have smirks on their faces as if they know something I don't. Suddenly, both boys are surrounding me; with Levi to my back and Christian facing me. Out of nowhere, Christian's fingers are tickling me, while Levi holds my arms so that I don't move. As I laughing and plead for them to stop, Mason's question is what breaks me out of my fit of laughter; "Why didn't you say anything about it being your birthday before?"

"I didn't think it'd mean anything to any of you, honestly." I mumble but I know they heard because dad embraces me in a tight hug. "Never. Anything about you means something to me" he says in a voice that leaves no room for discussion.

Not use to so much affection for the boys and dad, I differ the topic. "So, breakfast anyone?"

~

After breakfast, the boys and wishing me happy birthday, we settled that we'd go out for dinner in honor of my birthday anywhere I wanted. Given the opportunity, I'd go with In-N-Out any day, but that's not the case today; So, I choose my favorite restaurant that's Asian cuisine, that'd I'd only go a handful a times with my mom and grandma.

Having a lot of time to myself, I go to the library where I know no one will go but me. Until, Leo comes in through the door while turns back to see if any of the boys or dad saw him come in. At least that what I think. Once the door is closed and no one saw him, does he turn to face me with a wide grin on his face.

"Heard it was someone's birthday. Do you know who's it is? Could they be in here?" He says playfully with his to his brows as if look for something.

I roll my eyes at his antics, but can't hold back my smile from making a surprise appearance. "Hm, who's ever could it be?" I look from side to side playing along with him. "Oh, wait it's mine."

"Yeah, it is yours" he says while looking at me. I guess when he feels likes he's stared at me for too long he continues, "Anyways, I heard it was your birthday and I know how hard today is without being with you mom or grandma, so..."

At the mention of my mom and grandma, I feel a shift in my mood. I hadn't thought about them since the morning; at this, it makes me feel guilty (for having thought of them as I'd they were an afterthought).

They were everything to me. Still are everything to me.

"so, I have something for you. Here," finishes Leo. He hands me one small box and a velvet jewelry box.

"You didn't have to get me anything, Leo. I didn't expect you too, but thank you" I tell him giving him a genuine smile. "It's nothing, just open it."

As I open the small box, is a small jewelry box with a picture of my mom, grandma, and I together. I look to Leo speechless, he then nods gesturing to the other box. I open that one too, and inside is necklace. It's so beautiful.

"Thank you, Leo. This means a lot to me. Everything is beautiful" I say. Before he can manage to get a word out, I lunge at him throwing my arms around his neck after setting the gifts aside.

"No problem. I wanted to get you something small. Anyways, I got to get going, my mom must be looking for me," Leo tells me. He goes to the door, yet before he walks out he turns around with a smile and waves goodbye.

~

Everything went fine at dinner. We ordered a lot of food. It was actually fun. I got presents from the boys and dad, which was nice of them.

Once in my room, I get my picture of my mom, grandma and me from my nightstand and just hold it to my chest. This year's birthday was definitely different then pasta one. Especially with my mom and grandma not being by my side. I miss them a lot. I miss them everyday. Before going to sleep, I say one thing that I've been holding back all day.

"I wish both of you could have been with me today."

~

~

~

^ the necklace I envisioned Leo giving Kyla as a present

A/N: Hello, everyone!!! This chapter was so exciting to write. I tried to write this chapter so that it'd posted before my birthday, but I only managed to finish today (on my birthday). With that aside....

I hope you enjoyed reading :)

Chapter 25 - Change

✱ this chapter is like a week after chapter 24*

~ POV: Kyla Bower ~

Not much as happened recently... well other than I've gotten a little closer with the boys and dad. I guess after telling them the truth about my mom and grandma must have, kinda flipped a switch in them. It's actually kinda of nice.

Ryder is still the same with me, only a little more clinger; but I don't mind. Elijah gives a silent presence when he hangs around me even if I don't do anything. Levi, accompanies me in the library when I'm reading sitting in silence as we read. Christian is a more present and forthcoming with me, which I like that he does. Still, with Mason, I don't get him.

Mason hasn't really changed a lot, other than he hasn't made any snarky comment about me. It's just awkward with him in general now.

A couple days ago, Ryder, Levi and me were lounging in the game room when Mason walked in. I didn't pay too much to what he was doing; Ryder and me were playing speed with a deck of cards we had found when he seat to the side of me and Ryder. At some point, he even helped me win a round.

At this moment, I'm in the kitchen baking cupcakes. I had this sudden urge earlier to bake something, anything. I saw in the pantry we had the ingredients to make cupcakes so here I am; making a batch of cupcakes. Ryder was suppose to help me but he went out with his friends, which I don't mind.

In the of making the batter for the cupcakes, Leo waltzes in the kitchen causally coming to my side. "I didn't know you baked. What are you making?"

"I like baking, I just don't do it often is all. And I'm making cupcakes," I tell him.

Leo starts grabbing the dirty dishes and ingredients, I no longer need but to quick try to put a stop to him. "You don't need to do that you know" I tell him.

"I know I just want too" I replies instantly.

With Leo's help, we finish the cupcakes pretty quickly and place them in the oven. In the meantime, I start to make the frosting for it with Leo still next to me leaning on the kitchen island.

We talk about random things, when Mason walks into the kitchen. As he notices both, Leo and I, being close in distance he raises an eyebrow in questioning.

On the other hand, I try to act as if he hadn't enter the kitchen, and that it's still just me and Leo.

Mason must have noticed what I was doing because he comes up to us and gets right in the middle to open a cabinet to retrieve nothing and goes to sit on one of the stools from the kitchen counter.

With his presence, it makes the atmosphere rise with awkwardness and discomfort.

"So what's going on? Hmm?" Mason inquires.

"Nothing really. Just here spending sometime with Kyla" Leo replies to him.

"I think your mom was looking for you to help her with something, Leo. You should go see what it is she wants" Mason says with a glare directed to Leo.

What the fuck is Mason's problem?

Leo's whole demeanor shifts with Mason's comment. With a small 'see you later,' he walks out of the kitchen. I force my gaze to Mason who triumphantly relishes in the Leo's departure, but I won't put up with this bullshit.

"Why'd you do that?" I ask Mason narrowing my eyes at him.

"Do what? He needed to leave" he says blatantly.

I am done with his shit. He's taken it too far. First, he acted like I was nothing and now he's he deciding who I can't be in accompany with.

"What the hell is your problem with me? I haven't done anything to you and your acting like a man child throwing a tantrum on me like if I was a toy. We aren't anything. You can't decide things for me, any of you; but especially you. You treating me like dirt from the moment I first walked in to this house" I go on to tell him while he just says quite. I feel my throat bob up and down and I swallow the lump growing in my throat as I continue to spat at Mason.

"You guys are still barely getting to know me, and we're heading in the right path. But there's still so much between us, all of us. I've been pretty fine taking care of myself, considering that my mom is dead" I say.

Mason remains quiet. Since he clearly has nothing to say, I put that cupcakes that I had taken out of the oven into the fridge, and run from Mason. But I accidentally let a small sob escape me while trying to get away from Mason with the back of my arm.

~

In the confinement of my room, I blankly stare at the wall next to my bed. There's a knock at my door but I don't bother to say anything; another knock is heard. Still giving no answer, the door creaks open letting me know someone's inside. Don't they understand when someone wants to be alone. I immediately assume it's Ryder trying to get me to hang out with him.

"Look, Ryder, nows not a good time—," I say.

"You see that would've worked if it was Ryder. But I'm not Ryder" says Mason. Upon hearing his voice, I whip my around to look at him.

"I came to tell you I-I'm sorry. I didn't mean to make you feel less than you are. There's no excuse what I said or did in the past when you first came. I was an asshole to you. I wish I could take all the dumb shit that did to you, but I can" he says that last part in a low voice. Upon hearing him apologize, I stay quiet. I never would have expected an apology from Mason at all, from the others, yes.Locking his eyes with me he continues talking.

"I want to change with you. I will. I'm sorry about your mom and gran dma... I know a sorry doesn't count a lot but I'm sorry. And I want you to know I'm always here if you need me. Your my little sister," he tells me quietly.

My little sister.

Stunned from his words, I stay speechless. He considers me his sister. I look at him again and give him a small smile. I looked in his eyes to see if there was any chance of finding something but all I was was that he was being genuine.

"So I'll leave you now. See you at dinner, I have homework to do," with that he left.

~

Later at dinner, Mason sat in front of me. When Ryder was trying to get me break with his horrible jokes, Mason simply told him to shut the hell up; and with a smirk my way. Besides that everything was normal. How it should be.

If it's not it could last.

Chapter 26 - School

~ POV: Richard Bower ~

"Thank you so much for your time" I said to Mr. Thomas, the principal of Rhodes Academy.

Everything at home was going better than it was from the beginning. It was great. But not long after...

From the moment, I had even mention retiring to school, Kyla was not thrilled at all. She pouted like a little child. Kyla had to go to school; I had allowed for her to take sometime off, of school during to our family matters. however with things getting better at home that time off from school has long expired. I had her enrolled in the same school that Levi, and Mason had went to, where Ryder stills attends to finish his last year.

Rhodes Academy was a great school, where I knew that Kyla, along with my other children would flourish and excel. They deserved the best of the best in my opinion, and the best school for the, to attend to was Rhodes.

~

Next day...

~ POV: Kyla Bower ~

Today was going to be my first day at my new school. Yeah, no. It's not that I didn't want to go to school, I actually do. The thing is that this is a whole new environment where most people could simply judge me, just by taking a single glance in my direction. That's something I had kept to myself, the only person I told was my best friend Carter, but he had only tried to assure me that things would turn out to be okay.

So, being in my most school appropriate attire: a pair of cargo beige pants, loose long-sleeve brown shirt and my beat-up converse, at the dinner table playing with my breakfast seemed like a better option to pass my time. I was done trying to eat food, when I was all over the place just because of school. I guess from seeing how I was acting, Christian, must have gotten the memo that I needed any form of help, so that I could get over my "fear" of being the new kid at school, as the boys were putting it.

Clearing his throat, Christian, began what he had initially wanted to say from the beginning. "Come, on twins, we should be heading out, so that that you have time before classes start."

Also, did I fail to mention that they had all, the boys, taken a sort of liking to refer to Ryder and me as twins? No, well, they did. Since Ryder and I had so many similarities to the way we acted a little and what we liked, along with how we just sometimes knew what we needed from one another, they found that we acted like twins that were separated from birth. I think the only reason they think that is because we are so close of age, but they seem to have none of my reasons. In fact, it only amuses them even more.

Swinging my feet exasperatedly, I stand to go gather my backpack. I take my sweet time going up the stair but when I'm out of sight, I book it to my room, not wanting to waste valuable time. When I see the time, after getting my things I stare wide-eyed and make a beeline to the garage; If I don't get down now, late. I won't be late for classes, I'll just be late to some exploring I had planned before classes started at 8:45 am.

When Christian, Ryder, and me are situated inside the car, we drive off. But, of course, it wouldn't be a normal car ride, if Ryder didn't hog the music

Once in front of the school, that looks more like a castle, students' busy themselves going inside. Ryder heads in before me, while I stay back to take in the view and my surrounding. Just as I'm about to go inside, I accidentally bump into two people. "Oh, God. I'm so, so, so sorry," I say as I grab my backpack from the ground.

"It's ok," a familiar voice says from above me. Straightening, I see that it's Leo; who offers me a wide, welcoming smile.

"Your sorry? Please, you probably bumped into us on purpose. You ruined my new shoes!" this girl that's on the side says. She has dark hair, green eyes, and tall, wearing a really short skirt and white top.

"I really didn't see you guys. I'm sorry, I'll clean your shoes for you if," I say but am obnoxiously cut off by the girl. "Your sorry is worth shit," she shouts louder, that captures the attention of other students. "She said she's sorry," Leo tries to defend me.

The girl dramatically rolls her eyes and stomps off. The bell rings and all the students make their way to their classes. I thank and say goodbye to Leo. I make my way to the office to get my schedule, to my relief I find easily. The nice secretary who introduced herself as, Mrs. Moore, escorted me to my first class.

~

So far my classes have been going better than fine. My schedule is pretty standard: first period is English, then Musics/Arts, after Physics, History,

Foods and Nutrition, free period, and Calculus. So far my favorite classes are Musics/Arts and my free period obviously. It's lunch right now. Trying to find the cafeteria, I'm minding my own business when I suddenly get yanked from my forearm into the girls' restroom. I get whiplash as I turn to see who pulled me, it's the girl from the morning who I accidentally bumped into, and some other girls who must be her friends. "Look, I don't know what's going on but-" I start to question why I'm here, when she basically shuts me up with a zip motion with her hands to her mouth.

"I'm going to be doing the talking!" she whines like a five-year old." You made me look helpless in front of Ryder with my shoes, because of you he had to see me with my old shoes," she goes on. I swear she's complaining about some shoes that got one dirt on it, and impressing Ryder than other things that could be important; her voice is annoyingly pitchy that it makes me tone her out and not listen to any other word, she says.

She must have noticed at some point during her tantrum, that I wasn't paying attention to her that she grabs me roughly from the chin; just so I can see her. "Listen, and listen to me good, because I don't want to repeat myself... Ryder is mine, you understand. MINE! Look his way, get near him, or anything with him, and you pay" she warns. I still don't even know her name, and before I even have a change to think about it, I blurt out, "What's your name?"; which enraged her more then her messed up shoes.

Suddenly, her hand connects with my cheek. When I bring my eyes to look at her she's breathing hard, then signals her friends with her eyes in my direction. Abruptly, I'm pushed forward, followed by a couple of kicks to my side by the girls; I cover my face to avoid getting hurt in my eyes or nose. I loose time of how long they've been kicking me, when the lunch bell rings, alerting students go get to their next class, making the girls stop.

"Remember what I said, and follow them if you're wise enough too. And my name's Rose, just so you know next time," she says at the door of the bathroom just before she leaves. After Rose and her friends leave, I pick myself up and my belongs and go to class like if nothing happened wincing.

~

Instead of going to my next class, foods and nutrition, I go to the music room, where I know no one will find me. I want to be alone, where I know no one will kick me around, or bother me. Ryder and Leo are probably having a better time than I am with their friends, by not getting bullied over stupid things, like Rose did to me. My dad or Christian, Elijah, Levi, or Mason will probably get a call from the school, letting them know I didn't go to the rest of my classes. But I'll deal with that when it comes. I go to sit at the piano, and stare at the keys. My eyes get blurry with unshed tears, when one tears runs down my cheek, one after the other.

I will my hands to the piano keys and just let it all out.

Being stuck in the music room, time passed slow that when the last bell of the school rings, I grab my backpack from my side and walk out to the school quietly and slow. My body hurts, but what hurts the most is how they pushed me around like if I was no one, not a person.

Elijah is picking Ryder and me up. When I see his car, I slide into the back set and pull my knees up to my chin and stare blankly as everything passes by. I can feel Ryder's and Elijah's concerned eyes but I don't let it get to me.

I just want to go home

~

~

Chapter 27 - Seeing things

~ POV: Elijah Bower ~

When Kyla came back from school, just from looking at her, I knew something was not right... Or rather something had happened to her making her not her usual self. She wouldn't tear her eyes from the car's window. When Ryder or me, asked her questions about her first day at school, all she gave were one-worded answers. I thought we were progressing with her, or at least that she talked to me more than she was right now. A minute had not passed from when we arrived home to when I put the car in park, when Kyla bolted running; Ryder followed her with me in tow.

"Kyla!" I called out. "Kyla, wait!" went Ryder, but it was useless. She did not listen to us. She just continue to run to her room, slamming the door and locking herself within. With a sigh, I stared frowning at her door. Hopelessly, thinking that if I look enough she'll open the door and share a piece of what happened today at school with me.

Ryder placed his hand on my shoulder gesturing me to follow him. Aimlessly, I followed him downstairs to the kitchen, where I sat down at the kitchen island. Ryder had grab two glasses of water for the both of us. With a small sad smile, I accept it from him yet not moving to consume it. "Hey...

I'll find out what happened with Kyla at school. Promise," he assured me. "Thanks, Ry, but you don't have too. She'll come around eventually," I said more to myself.

"It's okay. I care about her too, if in any case something bad happened... I want to know, so that I she can know I'll have her back," he said. Hearing how he wanted to be close to her warmed my heart. "So how was your day?" I asked him/

For what seemed like more than a couple of minutes, Ryder proceeded to tell me about everything he could. From his friends, to upcoming plans, his classes and teacher, lunch, to new rising high school drama.

"All this happened, just today?" Some of the things he told me amazed me, it's not as different as how it was when I went of course, but hearing what some teens did and said was. "It's wild. Jesse and Matt hooking up wasn't even a big deal, but the argument between Lina and Taylor was! And it was stupid too, it was over there dad's job and who has the most things" he said exasperated. I just shook my head, still quite not believing what he said. Kyla still had not come out of her room, but Ryder and me wouldn't push her. "Come on dude, gotta do your homework remember," I remind him. "Yup, I'll get it on with it later" he says. "You better. I know you'll leave it until the very last minute, but get it over with."

When dinnertime comes by, I rush to be the first there to see that Kyla comes down. Slowly one by one, my brothers' come following Kyla after, with dad last. We eat in silence for a bit. A couple of bites in, and I look around the table to look at everyone. Dad, Ryder, and Levi are engrossed in a conversation of something that I don't know of, Christian and Mason are talking about college and some professors; while Kyla acts like she's listening to Christian and Mason's conversation, but she's starting intently as she moves her food around her plate with her fork. She must feel me staring because she stops moving her fork and looks directly at me as she cocks her head to one side.

I mouth to her that we need to talk, I don't expect her to react in any particular way; but when she mouths an okay and nods, I smile just a smidge. She smiles back at me yet before she gets the chance to look away, I catch sight of an angry shade of pink on her cheek under her eye. Squinting my eyes to catch a better look, to see that what I saw was actually there, I know that I am indeed not seeing things.

It looks like she got slapped or hit on the face.

What the fuck.

~ POV: Kyla Bower ~

When dinner is done, I think that I can save myself from the foreseeing headache I am most definitely going to be getting from Elijah... If only I manage to get my room fast from him, or before he can stop me from getting myself to the door of my room. Washington my plate quickly than I have ever done, I speed to get to the stair; but to my dismay, a hand grabs my upper arm from moving another step on the stairs. I jump from being startled and scared at the same time. I really thought I saved myself from Elijah.

He frowns knowing how startled I was, not expecting him. Yet, then again I did promise him we'd talk, I was just being a little shit that honestly didn't want to talk about to today. Still, I know we talk and that I would make an effort to open up to them. So... this is a step. A small, tiny baby step in the right directions. And on the other hand, I know that I cannot keep this bottled up.

"Hey, I thought we'd talk after dinner" he says softly.

"I know" I say dejectedly.

"And, you sort of promised me too..." he adds. Like I didn't already know and feel guilt about it now.

"Yeah. I know that too" I only say. Seeing that I don't really want to talk about this with him, he pulls me away a little and we walk together with him holding my hand as I walk behind him. We go up the stairs, but not to my room; but to his room. We don't go inside, but at the door he lets go of my hand and goes into his room to grab something. Before I have a chance to enter his room, say tells me to wait. When he's done getting something from his room that I cannot see, he grabs my hand again. He leads me downstairs where we were before, but this time we go together the door that goes outside where the pool is.

We go towards the side of the pool with the lounge chairs. I stare at him as he sets two chairs together by pulling them close to each other; he plants pillows on both chairs and a blanket on one. He guides me to one of the chairs where I then sit him following suit. He fixes the blanket on both of us so that we are covered and comfortable.

"Take a deep breath" He instructs me. Not really knowing what else to do, I trust what he is telling me and inhale a big breath of air.

"I'm here and I'm not going anywhere" he says almost in a whisper that I almost don't hear them.

I nod to his words, letting his words sink into my brain.

"Go on, whenever you're ready" he tells he softly.

Unknowingly holding my breath, I exhale and begin to tell him everything that happened at school, in the bathroom. With him, just listening intently to me, catching every word, I say.